Stories of Bearing

Stories of Bearing

Lives Under Moral Weight

G. C. SMITH

RESOURCE *Publications* • Eugene, Oregon

STORIES OF BEARING
Lives Under Moral Weight

Resource Publications
An Imprint of Wipf and Stock Publishers
199 W. 8th Ave., Suite 3
Eugene, OR 97401

www.wipfandstock.com

PAPERBACK ISBN: 979-8-3852-7784-1
HARDCOVER ISBN: 979-8-3852-7785-8
EBOOK ISBN: 979-8-3852-7786-5

VERSION NUMBER 03/11/26

For those who have carried moral weight quietly.

For the ones who stayed longer than they should have because leaving felt like betrayal.
For the ones who spoke and paid for it.
For the ones who left without being able to explain why.

For caregivers who learned that presence is not the same as fixing.
For leaders who discovered that integrity has limits.
For congregants who remain faithful in communities that cannot yet speak honestly.

And for anyone who has wondered whether the cost they were carrying was real, or necessary, or theirs alone.

You were not imagining it.
You were bearing something that deserved to be named.

Contents

Author's Note

THESE STORIES ARE WORKS of fiction.

They are not case studies, transcripts, or disguised accounts of identifiable people or congregations. They are composites, shaped from many conversations, observations, and moments accumulated over years of pastoral ministry and clinical work. Details have been altered, roles reconfigured, timelines compressed. What has been preserved is not fact, but truth.

This book does not offer instruction or diagnosis. It bears witness.

The stories gathered here attend to the moral weight carried by people who are trying to live faithfully within institutions that are constrained, imperfect, and human. They are about endurance, silence, discernment, and the quiet cost of integrity. There are no heroes and no villains, only people doing their best with what they can see at the time.

If you recognize yourself in these pages, that recognition is intentional. If you do not, the stories still ask to be read slowly, with attention to what is being carried and by whom.

Nothing here resolves easily. That, too, is intentional.

These are stories of bearing.

HOW THIS BOOK FUNCTIONS AS A COMPANION

This collection of stories is intentionally written as a companion volume to *Bearing the Weight: Moral Injury, Public Witness, and Reformed Faithfulness* and *Beyond Burnout: A Clergy Care Handbook for Moral Injury and Faithful Discernment*. Together, the three books address moral injury from distinct but mutually reinforcing angles: theological, clinical, and narrative.

Bearing the Weight names the problem.

It offers a theological and ecclesial framework for understanding moral injury as a systemic and spiritual reality, especially within church life and public witness. It articulates how integrity is strained, compromised, or fractured when faithfulness is constrained by institutional processes, loyalty expectations, and moral ambiguity. That book gives readers language, categories, and theological grounding for recognizing moral injury beyond individual pathology.

Beyond Burnout offers tools for care.

Where *Bearing the Weight* provides conceptual clarity, *Beyond Burnout* translates that clarity into pastoral and judicatory practice. It equips leaders with diagnostic distinctions, discernment frameworks, and concrete practices for care that do not rush repair or mislabel moral injury as burnout, fatigue, or personal failure. It is practical, procedural, and explicitly oriented toward those responsible for clergy care and institutional oversight.

This book shows what moral injury feels like from the inside.

The stories in this collection inhabit the lived experience that the other two books describe and address. Rather than explaining moral injury, they embody it—showing how it unfolds slowly, often invisibly, through silence, accommodation, endurance, and constrained agency. The characters in these stories do not diagnose themselves. They do not use clinical language. They simply live inside the moral weight that the other books name.

Taken together, the three books form a coherent whole:

- *Bearing the Weight* gives readers language and theology
- *Beyond Burnout* gives leaders tools and practices
- This collection gives the church imagination and empathy

The fiction resists the temptation to instruct or resolve. It allows readers—especially clergy, judicatory leaders, and congregational leaders—to recognize themselves without being analyzed. Many will see their own stories here before they are ready to name them elsewhere.

For some readers, this book will be an entry point—an emotionally accessible way into conversations they have avoided. For others, it will function as a mirror, deepening and complicating what they already understand intellectually. For leaders using the other two books in study, supervision, or retreat settings, these stories provide narrative case material that makes abstract concepts concrete and ethically urgent.

Most importantly, this collection safeguards what the other two books insist upon: that moral injury cannot be addressed only through explanation or technique. It must also be witnessed. These stories offer that witness—quietly, faithfully, and without demanding resolution.

In that sense, this book does not repeat the arguments of *Bearing the Weight* or the guidance of *Beyond Burnout.* It completes them.

Together, the three works invite the church not merely to understand moral injury, but to recognize it, care for it, and—crucially—to stop asking those who carry it to do so alone.

STORY 1

After the Agenda

DANIEL ARRIVED EARLY, WHICH meant he arrived alone.

The building was quiet in the way institutional buildings often were before meetings: not empty, but holding its breath. The fluorescent lights in the hallway hummed faintly. Somewhere down the corridor a copier warmed itself, the low mechanical sound rising and falling like a sigh. Daniel paused at the water fountain, pressed the button, watched the stream arc and miss his mouth the first time. He wiped his chin with the back of his hand and straightened his jacket.

The conference room door was ajar. Inside, the table was already set. Name placards stood at each place, their black block letters facing inward, as if reminding the chairs who they were supposed to be. At the far end, a stack of agendas sat neatly aligned. Daniel resisted the urge to straighten them. He had learned, over time, which impulses were worth indulging and which ones only made the waiting longer.

He took his usual seat, halfway down the table on the left. Close enough to be heard if necessary, far enough not to be expected to lead. He placed his bag at his feet and laid his yellow legal pad in front of him. The pad was creased down the middle, folded and unfolded so many times it no longer lay flat. He pressed it with his palm, then set his pen carefully on top.

For a few minutes, he simply sat. He noticed the details the way he always did before meetings: the scuff on the baseboard near the door, the faint coffee ring on the table that never quite disappeared, the thermostat set too low for anyone's comfort. He noticed how his shoulders tightened when he thought about the agenda and loosened again when he told himself not to think about it yet.

People began to arrive in ones and twos. Greetings were exchanged quietly at first, then with more volume as the room filled. Someone joked about traffic. Someone else apologized for being late before they were actually late. Daniel nodded, smiled, murmured replies. He had perfected the art of being present without being porous.

The chair arrived last, brisk and purposeful, carrying her own folder rather than taking one from the stack. Daniel wondered, not for the first time, what it would be like to sit at the head of the table. He suspected the view would not be much different, but the responsibility would feel heavier simply because it had nowhere else to go.

The meeting was called to order. The opening prayer was brief, practiced, careful not to linger. Daniel bowed his head, listened for the familiar phrases. Gratitude. Wisdom. Guidance. He had once believed those words did something on their own. Now he believed they mattered only insofar as people were willing to carry them out of the room afterward.

They moved through the early items quickly. Approval of minutes. Reports from subcommittees. Language that had been drafted, revised, and softened until it could be read aloud without catching on anything sharp. Daniel made a few notes, mostly dates and initials. He underlined a sentence in one report, then crossed it out when he realized he could not articulate why it troubled him.

Halfway down the agenda, there it was. Not labeled boldly, not set apart. Just another line item, indistinguishable in font and spacing from the rest. Daniel felt his body respond before his mind did. A small tightening in his chest, the sense of something drawing inward.

He glanced around the table. No one else seemed to notice. Or perhaps they had, and simply did not show it.

The chair cleared her throat. "We have an update," she said. "Nothing requiring action today."

Daniel uncapped his pen.

The update was delivered in measured tones. Dates. Conversations. A summary of concerns phrased in the passive voice, as if they had arisen on their own. Daniel listened carefully, tracking what was said and what was not. He had been present for some of the conversations referenced. He knew how different they had sounded in the room where they took place.

He wrote a word in the margin of his pad, then drew a line through it. He wrote another, then folded the corner of the page down slightly, a habit he had picked up years ago when he needed to mark things he could not say.

The update concluded. The chair looked around the table. "Questions?"

The silence that followed was not empty. It was dense, layered with calculation and restraint. Daniel felt it settle over him, familiar as a coat he no longer noticed wearing.

He thought of the pastor. The way he had sat across from him, hands folded, voice steady but eyes tired. The sentence he had spoken, quietly, as if testing whether it could be said at all. Daniel had nodded then, had said something about taking time, about process. He had meant it. He still did.

But process, Daniel knew, was not neutral. It carried weight of its own.

He glanced down at his legal pad. His pen hovered just above the paper. He imagined asking the question that had formed in his mind, imagined the room's response. Not anger. Not dismissal. Something more subtle: the shift, the recalibration, the way the conversation would be redirected without appearing to be shut down.

He lowered his pen.

"No questions," someone said, and Daniel realized with a small start that it had been his own voice.

The chair nodded. "All right. Let's move on."

The agenda continued. Daniel followed along, attentive, engaged. He asked a question later about a budget line, one that was safe and necessary. He contributed a comment about scheduling that was received with appreciation. The meeting flowed as it always did, competent and contained.

Still, something had changed.

Daniel felt it as a slight dissonance, like a note held too long. He told himself it was fatigue. He told himself he had been doing this work for a long time. He told himself many things that had once been true and might still be, but no longer explained what he felt.

When the meeting adjourned, people gathered their belongings. Chairs scraped softly against the floor. Someone made another joke, this one about lunch. Daniel closed his legal pad and slipped it into his bag. As he stood, he noticed his hand tremble slightly. He clenched it, then relaxed it again.

In the hallway, the air felt cooler. The noise of the meeting room faded behind him. He took a step toward the exit, then stopped.

Down the corridor, near the windows, the pastor was standing alone.

Daniel hesitated. He did not yet know what he would say. He only knew that whatever he did say would matter more than anything he had written down that morning.

He started walking.

The pastor's name was Mark, though Daniel had learned long ago that names carried different weights depending on where they were spoken. In meetings, Mark was a line item, a situation, a matter requiring careful attention. In the small office where they had first talked, he had been a person who sat forward in his chair as if bracing himself against something invisible.

Daniel slowed his pace as he approached him now, aware of the way time seemed to thicken in moments like this. The hallway was long and narrow, the windows on one side letting in a pale afternoon light that flattened everything it touched. Mark stood with his back to the glass, his reflection faintly visible, as if another version of him were watching from behind.

"Hey," Daniel said, stopping a few feet away.

"Hey," Mark replied. He smiled, a practiced thing, polite and careful. "I wasn't sure if you'd be out yet."

Daniel nodded. "We just wrapped up."

They stood there, neither of them moving closer. Daniel noticed the folder tucked under Mark's arm, its edges worn soft. He wondered how many times Mark had carried it into rooms like this, hoping it might do some of the work for him.

"How did it go?" Mark asked, though his voice suggested he already knew the answer would be partial at best.

Daniel took a breath. He chose his words the way he always did in these moments, laying them out in his mind first, testing their weight. "It went as expected," he said again, hearing how it sounded now that he had said it twice in the same day.

Mark nodded slowly. "Right."

There was a pause. Daniel felt the urge to fill it, to offer something more, something reassuring. He resisted. He had learned that reassurance, given too quickly, often became another thing someone had to carry.

"They shared the update," Daniel continued. "No decisions today."

"Of course," Mark said. He shifted his weight from one foot to the other. "That's probably good."

"Probably," Daniel agreed.

They both knew what that word covered over.

Mark looked down at the floor, then back up. "I appreciate you being in the room," he said. "It helps to know someone's there who understands."

Daniel felt the familiar tightening in his chest. Understanding was a complicated thing. It implied alignment, or at least solidarity, and Daniel was never quite sure how much of either he was permitted.

"I'm glad to be there," he said. It was true, as far as it went.

Mark smiled again, this time with a flicker of something else underneath—weariness, perhaps, or disappointment held in check. "Well," he said, straightening. "I won't keep you."

Daniel watched him turn and walk down the hallway, his steps measured, unhurried. He noticed the way Mark held his shoulders, upright but not rigid, as if maintaining a posture he had learned to inhabit over time. Daniel wondered how long it could be sustained.

He waited until Mark was out of sight before moving himself. He headed for the stairwell instead of the elevator, needing the physical sensation of walking, of descending one step at a time. The stairwell smelled faintly of cleaning solution and old carpet. His footsteps echoed softly, a rhythm that steadied him.

As he descended, Daniel's mind replayed the update from the meeting. He could hear the phrases again, the careful wording, the omissions that had been framed as restraint. He tried to imagine what it would have sounded like if someone had spoken plainly. He could see the room tightening, the subtle shifts in posture, the way eyes would have moved toward the chair for cues.

He reached the ground floor and pushed through the heavy door into the lobby. The space was larger, brighter, with a reception desk that was now unoccupied. Daniel paused near the entrance, looking out through the glass at the parking lot beyond. Cars were scattered unevenly, some already gone, others lingering like he was.

He thought back to the first conversation he'd had with Mark, months earlier. Mark had arrived carrying the same folder, had placed it carefully on the table before opening it. He had spoken calmly at first, outlining the situation as if he were briefing Daniel on someone else's life. Then, midway through a sentence, his voice had faltered.

"I don't know how to do this anymore," Mark had said then, the words escaping before he could stop them. He had looked almost startled by his own honesty.

Daniel had listened, had nodded, had said the things he was expected to say. He had talked about process, about time, about patience. He had meant all of it. He had also known, even then, that none of it would resolve what Mark was carrying.

Outside, a gust of wind rattled the glass. Daniel zipped his jacket and stepped into the cold. The air was sharp, bracing. He breathed it in deeply, grateful for the clarity of the sensation.

As he walked toward his car, his phone buzzed in his pocket. He ignored it at first, then stopped and pulled it out. A message from the chair.

Thanks for your steady presence today, it read. Always helpful.

Daniel stared at the screen for a moment longer than necessary. He typed a reply, erased it, then typed a simpler one.

Glad to help, he sent.

He slipped the phone back into his pocket and continued to his car. The parking lot was quiet now, the earlier bustle gone. He unlocked the door and sat behind the wheel without starting the engine.

He thought about the phrase the chair had used: steady presence. It was meant as a compliment, and he took it as such. Still, he could not shake the sense that steadiness had become a kind of expectation, a way of describing someone who absorbed motion so that others did not have to.

He rested his forehead briefly against the steering wheel. The legal pad lay on the passenger seat, its yellow cover catching the light. He reached over and opened it, flipping past pages dense with notes until he reached the most recent one.

The date was there. Mark's initials. Nothing else.

Daniel considered adding a line, something that would remind him later of what this meeting had cost. He searched for words that would be both honest and harmless. He found none.

He closed the pad and placed it back on the seat. Outside, the sky was already beginning to darken, the light fading faster than he expected.

Daniel started the engine and pulled out of the lot, carrying with him the familiar, unspoken understanding that whatever came next—for Mark, for the committee, for the system—would arrive layered with the same careful language, the same practiced restraint.

And he would be there, steady as ever, bearing what could not be said aloud.

Daniel woke before his alarm, the room still dark, the house quiet in the way it was only before dawn. For a moment he lay still, listening. The refrigerator hummed faintly in the kitchen. Somewhere outside, a truck passed on the main road, its sound fading quickly. He closed his eyes again, but his mind was already moving.

He thought of the meeting room. The agenda. The word informational. He felt the familiar pull to rehearse what he might have said, how he might have framed it differently. He stopped himself. That exercise never led anywhere useful. It only sharpened the sense of what had already passed.

He swung his legs over the side of the bed and sat, elbows on his knees. His shoulders ached slightly, a dull reminder of tension carried without noticing. He stood and padded down the hallway to the kitchen, moving quietly out of habit, though no one else was there to wake.

Coffee first. Always.

As the machine sputtered to life, Daniel leaned against the counter and stared at the small stack of mail he had not yet sorted. Circulars. A handwritten envelope from an old colleague. He set it aside, unopened. There were days when even small connections felt heavier than he could manage.

He poured the coffee and took it into the living room, settling into the chair by the window. Outside, the sky was just beginning to lighten, the dark giving way reluctantly. He watched it change, the way he often did, not because it brought comfort, but because it required nothing from him.

His phone lay on the table beside the chair. He had not checked it yet, and he resisted the urge now. There would be messages. There were always messages. Some of them would ask things of him. Others would thank him for things he was no longer sure he should be thanked for.

He sipped the coffee, then set the mug down untouched.

Years earlier, when he had first taken on this role, he had believed clarity would come with experience. He had imagined that over time the right questions would become obvious, that the tension he felt in meetings was simply the friction of learning. Instead, the questions had multiplied, and the tension had changed shape. It no longer felt like uncertainty. It felt like knowledge with nowhere to go.

He thought again of Mark, standing in the hallway, the careful way he had asked how the meeting went. Daniel replayed the moment in his mind, the way he had answered. As expected. The phrase had felt insufficient even as he spoke it. Still, he had not known what else to say.

Daniel reached for his legal pad, which he had placed on the coffee table the night before without remembering doing so. He flipped it open to a blank page. The yellow paper stared back at him, patient and accusatory all at once.

He began to write, not notes exactly, but fragments. Phrases that came to him without effort.

Steady presence.

Process.

No action required.

He paused, pen hovering. He added another line.

Whose cost?

The question startled him with its directness. He underlined it once, then twice. He felt a small surge of something—recognition, perhaps, or relief at seeing the question in his own handwriting. It did not last.

He thought of the chair's message from the day before, the praise offered so casually. Always helpful. He wondered what, precisely, had been helpful. His silence? His compliance? The way he had absorbed the moment without disturbing the flow of the meeting?

Daniel closed the pad and leaned back in the chair. He pressed his fingers into his temples, feeling the pulse there. He told himself, not for the first time, that he was doing his job. That restraint was part of the role. That systems required patience.

He had said these things to others, often gently, often convincingly. They were not lies. They were also not the whole truth.

Later that morning, he found himself thinking of an earlier meeting, years ago, when he had spoken up. He could still picture the room, smaller than the one they used now, with windows that let in too much light. He had been less careful then, more certain that naming something plainly would be received as an act of faithfulness.

He had asked a question that cut too close to the center. He had watched as the room shifted, the collective posture adjusting almost imperceptibly. No one had rebuked him. No one had dismissed his concern. They had simply moved on, the conversation redirected with practiced ease.

Afterward, someone had taken him aside. "You're not wrong," they had said, voice low, confidential. "But you need to think about how things land."

Daniel had nodded, grateful for the guidance. It had taken him a long time to understand what was being offered. Not correction, exactly. Instruction.

Since then, he had learned to think constantly about how things landed. He had learned to anticipate the room's tolerance, to calibrate his words accordingly. He had learned which truths could be spoken safely and which ones required a different kind of stewardship.

He had also learned the cost of that stewardship, though he had not yet found a way to speak about it.

The phone buzzed again on the table, insistent now. Daniel picked it up. A message from Mark.

Thanks for checking in yesterday, it read. Let me know if there's anything I should be doing.

Daniel stared at the words. The request was reasonable. The expectation implicit. He typed a response, then erased it.

What could he say? Be patient. Trust the process. Take care of yourself. Each phrase felt thin, worn from use. He knew how they sounded from the other side.

He finally typed: I'll be in touch once there's more clarity.

He sent the message and set the phone face down.

The rest of the morning passed in a blur of small tasks. Emails answered. Forms reviewed. A brief call with a colleague who spoke enthusiastically about a new initiative. Daniel listened, offered affirmation where appropriate. He did not mention the meeting. He did not mention Mark.

By midday, the unease he had woken with had settled into something heavier, more diffuse. Not anxiety exactly. A sense of misalignment, like walking with a stone in his shoe and telling himself it was manageable.

He ate lunch at his desk, a sandwich he barely tasted. As he threw away the wrapper, he caught sight of his reflection in the darkened computer screen. For a moment, he did not recognize the man looking back at him. Not because he looked older, though he did, but because his expression was so carefully neutral.

Daniel leaned back in his chair and closed his eyes.

He wondered, with a clarity that did not bring comfort, how long he could continue to do this work without something in him hardening beyond repair. He wondered whether the steadiness others relied on was slowly hollowing him out.

He also knew, with equal clarity, that walking away would not be simple. It would not be clean. There were people—Mark among them—who were counting on him to remain where he was, to keep absorbing what the system could not.

The thought settled heavily.

When he opened his eyes again, the office was unchanged. The afternoon light slanted across the floor. Papers waited to be filed. Decisions waited to be deferred.

Daniel picked up his pen and returned to his work, carrying with him the unspoken question he had written that morning, now folded back into the legal pad, pressing faintly through the pages.

Whose cost?

It followed him through the day, unanswered, a weight he did not yet know how to set down.

The next meeting took place two weeks later, though it felt longer than that to Daniel. Time had a way of stretching around unresolved things, expanding to fill whatever space it was given. He arrived early again, though this time the building was not empty. Voices drifted down the hallway from another conference room. Laughter, brief and bright, followed by the scrape of chairs.

Daniel paused outside the familiar door and took a breath. He felt steadier than he had after the last meeting, which unsettled him. He had learned to distrust steadiness when it arrived too easily.

Inside, the table was arranged the same way. The agendas were stacked neatly, though he noticed the font had changed slightly. Someone had chosen a different template. He wondered who, and why. Small decisions like that often carried more meaning than anyone admitted.

As people filtered in, Daniel exchanged greetings, listened to comments about the weather, about travel, about a conference someone had attended. He nodded, smiled, took his seat. He placed his legal pad in front of him and this time did not bother pressing it flat.

The chair called the meeting to order. The opening prayer was longer than usual, or perhaps Daniel was only more aware of it now. He listened as words about discernment and courage were spoken aloud, their familiarity dulling their edge. He wondered, briefly, what would happen if someone took them seriously.

They moved through the agenda. The earlier items passed without incident. Daniel followed along, marking a few notes, responding when addressed. He felt himself slipping into the rhythm he knew so well, the one that allowed him to be present without being exposed.

When they reached the update again, Daniel's body reacted less sharply than before. The tightening in his chest was still there, but muted, as if his system had learned what to expect. He was not sure whether that was a relief or a warning.

The chair introduced the item. "There's been some movement," she said. "Nothing conclusive yet."

The update was longer this time. It included additional conversations, more context. It was still careful. Still partial. Daniel noticed the way certain words were repeated, the way responsibility was dispersed across unnamed forces. Circumstances. Dynamics. Concerns.

As the update continued, Daniel felt a thought forming, slow and deliberate. It was not a question exactly, more an observation. He could already hear how it would land. He could see the room responding, the way it always did, with polite attention followed by a redirection that would render the comment harmless.

He looked down at his legal pad. The words he had written that morning surfaced again in his mind. Whose cost?

Daniel raised his hand.

The chair paused, surprised but composed. "Yes, Daniel?"

He cleared his throat. He felt the eyes of the room settle on him, not hostile, not welcoming. Attentive. He chose his words carefully, aware that even care could be a kind of evasion.

"I'm struck," he said slowly, "by how much of this process depends on Mark continuing to hold things together while we sort through next steps. I wonder how we're accounting for the toll that's taking."

The room was very still.

Daniel could feel the moment tipping, balanced between acknowledgment and absorption. He had not accused. He had not demanded. He had simply named something that was already present.

The chair nodded. "That's an important consideration," she said. "And it's one we're holding."

Daniel waited. He did not speak again.

Another member leaned forward. "It's difficult," she said, "because we don't want to rush, and we also don't want to create expectations we can't meet."

"Yes," the chair agreed. "Exactly."

The conversation moved on.

Daniel felt something settle in his chest. Not relief. Not regret. Something closer to resignation, though even that felt too dramatic. He had spoken. The words had landed. And now they had been folded back into the system, neutralized without being dismissed.

He made no further comments during the meeting.

When adjournment came, the room emptied more quickly than usual. People seemed eager to move on, to reclaim the rest of the afternoon. Daniel gathered his things slowly, allowing others to pass him as they exited.

In the hallway, he hesitated, half-expecting to see Mark again. The corridor was empty.

He walked toward the stairs, his steps measured. With each one, he felt the weight of what he had done and not done settle more firmly. He had named the cost. He had not altered it.

Outside, the air was warmer than he expected. Spring was edging its way in, tentative but persistent. Daniel stood on the steps for a moment, letting the sun hit his face. He closed his eyes briefly, then opened them again.

His phone buzzed. A message from the chair.

Thank you for raising that point today, it read. It's helpful to keep those perspectives in mind.

Daniel stared at the screen. He could feel the familiar mixture of appreciation and emptiness that followed messages like this. He typed a response, then deleted it. He left the message unanswered.

As he walked to his car, he thought again of the meeting years ago when he had first learned how things landed. He wondered whether that lesson had finally reached its limit, or whether he was simply more aware of its cost now.

He unlocked the car and sat behind the wheel, hands resting loosely on the steering wheel. He did not start the engine right away. Instead, he reached for his legal pad and flipped to the page from that morning.

The words were still there, underlined twice. Whose cost?

Below them, he wrote another line.

Held.

He closed the pad and placed it on the passenger seat.

As he pulled out of the parking lot, Daniel felt the familiar steadiness return, settling over him like a practiced posture. He wondered, not for the first time, how long it could be maintained before it became indistinguishable from silence.

He drove on, carrying with him the quiet knowledge that speaking, even carefully, did not always lighten the load.

Sometimes it only clarified what would continue to be borne.

Daniel did not see Mark again for several weeks.

This was not unusual. The spaces between encounters often widened during periods like this, filled with updates delivered through intermediaries and decisions deferred in the language of caution. Daniel followed the developments as he always did, through summaries and emails that arrived carefully worded and lightly redacted by habit rather than intent.

Still, he noticed the absence.

He found himself scanning hallways when he entered the building, half-expecting to see Mark standing near the windows again, folder tucked under his arm. Each time the space was empty, Daniel felt a small, irrational sense of relief, followed quickly by something like regret.

When they did finally meet again, it was unplanned.

Daniel was leaving his office late one afternoon, the building already settling into evening quiet. He had stayed longer than usual, finishing a report that had taken more care than it should have. As he stepped into the elevator, the doors began to close, then opened again.

Mark slipped inside.

"Sorry," he said, breathless. "Didn't think I'd make it."

"No problem," Daniel replied. He pressed the button for the lobby.

The doors slid shut, and the elevator began its slow descent. The silence between them felt different here, enclosed and unavoidable. Daniel glanced at the mirrored wall and caught a glimpse of them together, standing side by side without the buffer of a table or agenda.

Mark looked tired. Not dramatically so, not in a way that would alarm anyone at a distance. But Daniel recognized the particular slackness around the eyes, the careful way Mark held himself upright, as if posture alone were doing the work of resolve.

"How are you holding up?" Daniel asked, surprised at himself for asking it so plainly.

Mark considered the question. The elevator hummed softly, the numbers ticking down.

"I don't know," he said finally. He smiled faintly, as if to soften the admission. "I keep thinking I should have a better answer by now."

Daniel nodded. "I've noticed that timelines don't always help with that."

Mark let out a quiet laugh. "That's one way to put it."

They descended another floor. Mark shifted his weight, then spoke again. "I heard you raised a question at the last meeting."

Daniel felt the familiar tightening, though it was less sharp this time. "Yes," he said. "I thought it was important to name."

"I appreciate it," Mark said. "Even if it didn't change anything."

Daniel studied his face, the way he said it without bitterness. "Sometimes naming is all that's possible in a given moment."

"I know," Mark replied. "I just wish it counted for more."

The elevator reached the lobby with a soft chime. The doors opened, releasing them into the wide, quiet space. They stepped out together and walked toward the exit.

Outside, the air was cool, the sky already darkening. Mark paused near the door, his hand resting briefly on the handle.

"I've been thinking about leaving," he said.

The words landed heavily between them.

Daniel did not respond right away. He felt the weight of the confession, the way it demanded care without urgency. He also felt the instinctive pull to say something reassuring, something that would steady the ground under Mark's feet.

He resisted.

"What has you thinking that?" he asked instead.

Mark looked out through the glass, as if the answer were written somewhere beyond the parking lot. "I don't think I can keep doing this without losing something I'm not willing to lose," he said. "I don't know if that means I'm failing, or just finally being honest."

Daniel swallowed. He recognized the terrain Mark was describing, the place where discernment stopped being abstract and began to feel like grief.

"Those aren't the only two options," Daniel said quietly.

Mark nodded. "I know. But they're the ones that show up first."

They stood there for a moment longer, neither of them moving. Daniel felt the limits of what he could offer pressing in. He was not Mark's supervisor. He was not the one who would decide what came next. He could not promise protection or clarity.

He could bear witness.

"Whatever you decide," Daniel said, choosing each word carefully, "it doesn't erase the faithfulness of what you've already carried."

Mark turned to look at him. His eyes were bright, though he did not cry. "I hope that's true," he said.

"I believe it is," Daniel replied.

Mark exhaled slowly, as if releasing something he had been holding. "Thank you," he said. "For listening. For being honest, even when it's quiet."

Daniel felt a tightening in his chest, different from the ones that usually accompanied these conversations. He nodded once, unable to say more without tipping into something he did not yet have language for.

They parted at the door, Mark stepping out into the evening, Daniel remaining inside. He watched as Mark crossed the parking lot, his figure growing smaller with each step. He wondered whether this was the last time they would speak like this, without intermediaries or minutes taken.

As Daniel walked back to his office to gather his things, he felt the familiar steadiness return, but it was altered now, threaded with something else. He thought of the chair, of the committee, of the careful pace of process. He thought of the question he had asked in the meeting, and the way it had been absorbed.

He also thought of Mark's words: losing something I'm not willing to lose.

At his desk, Daniel gathered his bag and legal pad. He hesitated, then opened the pad to the most recent page. Beneath the words he had written earlier, he added another line.

Bearing has limits.

He closed the pad.

As he turned off the light and stepped into the hallway, Daniel felt the weight of that sentence settle into him. Not as a directive, not as a solution, but as a truth that would need to be carried alongside the others.

Outside, the night had fully arrived. Daniel pulled his jacket tighter and walked to his car, aware that whatever came next—for Mark, for the system, for himself—would require a different kind of attention.

One that could no longer be sustained by steadiness alone.

The letter arrived on a Thursday.

Daniel recognized the return address before he opened it. The handwriting was Mark's—neat, deliberate, the kind that suggested the writer had taken time to be legible even when saying something difficult. Daniel stood at the kitchen counter with the envelope in his hand longer than necessary, the late afternoon light slanting through the window, catching the dust in the air.

He opened it carefully, as if the paper might tear more easily than it should.

The letter was not long. Mark had never been one for excess. He wrote plainly about discernment, about conversations that had clarified rather than resolved. He named gratitude without sentimentality and grief without accusation. He spoke of leaving not as escape, but as an acknowledgment of limits reached honestly.

Daniel read the letter twice.

When he finished, he folded it and set it on the counter. He rested his hands flat against the cool surface and let the weight of it settle. He had known this was coming. That did not make it lighter.

Later that day, the chair called.

"I wanted you to hear from me directly," she said, her voice careful but warm. "Mark has let us know he'll be stepping away at the end of the quarter."

"Yes," Daniel said. "He wrote."

There was a pause. Daniel could hear papers shifting on the other end of the line, the subtle sounds of someone preparing to say the right thing.

"We're framing this as a mutual discernment," the chair continued. "An honest recognition that the season has run its course."

Daniel closed his eyes. "That seems appropriate."

"We'll need your help," she added. "With the messaging. Making sure the community understands."

Daniel opened his eyes again and looked out the window. The sky was overcast now, the earlier light gone. "I can help with that," he said. He meant it, even as he felt the familiar pull of something tightening inside him.

After the call ended, Daniel sat down at the small table by the window. He took out his legal pad and opened it to a fresh page. The yellow paper felt both inviting and accusatory, as it always did when something important needed to be named.

He wrote Mark's name at the top.

Beneath it, he wrote a list of tasks. Draft statement. Timeline. Care plan. Each item was necessary. Each one felt insufficient.

He stared at the page, then turned back a few pages to where he had written Bearing has limits. He traced the words with his finger, feeling the faint indentation left by the pen.

Over the next weeks, the work unfolded as it always did. Meetings were scheduled. Language was refined. A statement was circulated, revised, approved. Daniel participated fully, offering suggestions, smoothing phrases, ensuring that what was said could be received without provoking unnecessary alarm.

The announcement was made on a Sunday morning. Daniel did not attend the service, but he imagined it easily enough: the careful tone, the measured words, the way gratitude and sadness would be balanced just so. He imagined Mark standing at the front, composed, offering thanks. He imagined the congregation listening, nodding, absorbing the information without yet feeling its weight.

In the days that followed, messages arrived. Some were kind. Some were confused. A few were sharp, their questions edged with disappointment. Daniel answered what he could, deferred what he could not. He found himself once again praised for steadiness, for clarity, for being a calming presence in a time of transition.

He accepted the praise with practiced ease.

One evening, near the end of the quarter, Daniel and Mark met one last time. They chose a small café halfway between their offices, a place neither of them frequented. It was quiet, the late hour thinning out the crowd.

They sat across from each other, mugs between their hands.

"I wanted to thank you," Mark said. "For staying in it with me."

Daniel nodded. "I wish it hadn't cost what it did."

Mark smiled faintly. "Everything costs something."

They sat in silence for a moment, the clink of dishes and low murmur of other conversations filling the space.

"I don't know what comes next," Mark said. "And I'm trying to let that be okay."

Daniel considered him, the way he looked lighter and more burdened all at once. "Not knowing isn't the same as being lost," he said. "Even if it feels like it."

Mark nodded. "That's what I'm telling myself."

They parted outside the café, exchanging a brief, unadorned goodbye. Daniel watched as Mark walked away, then turned in the opposite direction.

Weeks later, the committee met again. Mark's name no longer appeared on the agenda. Other matters took its place, urgent and complex in their own ways. Daniel noticed the absence like a missing tooth, something his tongue returned to again and again without thinking.

As the meeting progressed, he felt the familiar steadiness settle over him. He listened, spoke when necessary, remained silent when it was not. The work continued, as it always did.

At the end of the meeting, as people gathered their things, the chair lingered. "I just wanted to say," she said, "you handled all of that with a lot of grace."

Daniel smiled. "We all did what we could."

He walked out of the building into the late afternoon light. The air was warm, the kind of warmth that suggested summer was on its way. He stood for a moment, letting the sun hit his face, feeling the quiet satisfaction of a season brought to a close.

And yet.

As he walked to his car, Daniel felt the accumulation of what had been borne settle more heavily than before. Not just Mark's story, but the pattern it fit into. The way faithfulness had been named and contained, the way cost had been acknowledged just enough to move forward.

He sat behind the wheel without starting the engine. He reached for his legal pad and flipped through it slowly, page by page. Names. Dates. Questions half-asked and fully withdrawn. He stopped at a blank page near the back.

He wrote one final sentence.

This, too, has been carried.

He closed the pad and set it on the seat beside him.

Daniel did not know how much longer he would do this work. He did not yet know what it would mean to set some of this weight down. He only knew that bearing had shaped him, quietly and profoundly, and that whatever came next would have to reckon with that truth.

He started the engine and pulled out of the lot, carrying with him not resolution, but clarity.

And for now, that would have to be enough.

STORY 2

The Sabbatical Letter

THE LETTER BEGAN, AS so many things did now, with gratitude.

I am deeply thankful for the gift of sabbatical...

Rachel typed the sentence, read it once, then again. She left it there longer than she meant to, the cursor blinking at the end like it was waiting for her to continue. Outside the study window, the afternoon light slanted across the bare branches of the maple tree, catching on the last stubborn leaves that hadn't fallen in autumn. They rattled faintly in the wind.

She deleted the sentence.

Rachel leaned back in her chair and closed her eyes. The room still smelled faintly of coffee, though the mug beside her keyboard had gone cold hours ago. She had returned from sabbatical three weeks earlier. Long enough, she thought, that she should have found her footing by now.

Everyone expected her to be refreshed.

They had said it in emails before she left, their words warm and confident. *You'll come back renewed. Take the time you need. We can't wait to see what God does in this season.*

She had believed them. Or at least she had wanted to.

The sabbatical itself had been quiet. No dramatic revelations, no sudden healing. She had slept. Walked. Read novels she hadn't had the patience for in years. She had stopped waking in the night with a tightness in her chest she could never quite explain. She had felt her body settle, inch by inch, into something like ease.

And then, somewhere in the middle of all that rest, clarity had arrived.

Not clarity about what to do next. Not answers. Just a stark, unyielding awareness of how much she had been carrying, and how little of it had ever been named. She had seen, with an almost painful sharpness, the places where she had learned to bend herself into shapes that fit the institution more easily than they fit her conscience.

The clarity had not felt like freedom. It had felt like standing in a cleared field with no shelter.

Now, back in her study, Rachel stared at the blank screen. The letter was supposed to be simple. A sabbatical report. A reflection. Something she could share with the session, with the committee, with the people who had prayed for her while she was gone.

She typed again.

This time away has given me space to reflect. . .

She paused. Reflected on what? She could hear the expected conclusions already, the phrases she herself had used with other pastors returning from leave. New energy. Renewed vision. A deeper sense of calling.

None of those felt true.

Rachel rubbed her eyes and glanced at the calendar on the wall. Meetings were starting to stack up again. Catch-up conversations. Gentle check-ins. Everyone asking, in their own way, whether she was ready to be back.

She thought of the first Sunday she had returned to the pulpit. The sanctuary had felt both familiar and strange, the faces turned toward her with unmistakable affection. She had preached carefully that day, choosing a text that allowed for reflection without confession. People had lined up afterward, smiling, hugging her, telling her how good it was to have her back.

"You look rested," one woman had said, squeezing her hand.

Rachel had smiled and thanked her. The truth—that she felt clearer but also more brittle than before—had lodged in her throat, unsayable.

Back at the computer, she typed another sentence.

I am grateful for the rest, even as I continue to discern its meaning.

She read it twice. It sounded vague enough to pass. It also felt like a betrayal of something she could not yet articulate.

Rachel pushed back from the desk and stood. The study was small but orderly, bookshelves lining one wall, her ordination certificate framed and hanging slightly crooked. She crossed the room and straightened it, then laughed softly at herself. Old habits returned easily.

She moved to the window and rested her forehead against the glass. Outside, a neighbor walked a dog down the sidewalk, the leash slack between them. The dog stopped to sniff at something invisible, unconcerned with destination.

During sabbatical, Rachel had imagined this moment differently. She had imagined returning with stories, insights, a renewed sense of purpose she could offer generously. Instead, she felt like she was carrying something fragile and sharp-edged, unsure where to place it without causing damage.

Her phone buzzed on the desk behind her. She did not turn around right away. Eventually, she picked it up and glanced at the screen.

A message from the clerk of session.

Hope you're settling back in well. Looking forward to your sabbatical reflections when you're ready.

When you're ready.

Rachel set the phone down without responding. She knew the clerk meant well. Everyone did. That was part of what made this so difficult. There was no antagonist here, no one to resist. Only a system that knew how to receive certain kinds of stories and not others.

She returned to her chair and stared again at the letter. The cursor blinked patiently.

She thought of something she had written in her journal during sabbatical, a sentence she had circled and underlined without knowing why at the time.

Rest didn't fix this. It just made it impossible to ignore.

Rachel hovered her fingers over the keyboard, then slowly typed the sentence into the letter. She read it once and felt her breath catch.

She deleted it immediately.

The room felt suddenly smaller, the air heavier. She closed the document without saving and sat back, hands folded in her lap.

The letter would have to wait.

She knew, with a quiet certainty that unsettled her, that the problem was not finding the right words. It was finding a place where the words could be received without being reshaped into something safer.

Outside, the last of the leaves broke free from the tree and skittered across the yard. Rachel watched them for a moment longer, then turned back to her desk, already aware that whatever came next would require a different kind of courage than rest alone could provide.

Rachel avoided the letter by doing everything else.

She answered emails she could have postponed. She reorganized her bookshelves, reshelving volumes she had not touched in years, convincing herself she might soon. She agreed to coffee with a colleague who wanted to hear about sabbatical, though she kept her account deliberately shallow: the walking trails, the novels, the relief of sleeping through the night.

"You sound good," her colleague said, smiling. "Clear."

Rachel nodded. She had learned that clear was a word people used when they wanted reassurance without detail.

At night, she lay awake again—not from exhaustion, but from a low, persistent alertness that had nothing to do with stress and everything to do with honesty. The clarity sabbatical had brought had not faded with her return. If anything, it had sharpened. She could feel it now in meetings, in conversations, in the pulpit. Words that once slid past her now caught.

The first session meeting after her return was cordial, even warm. People thanked her for her sermon. They asked gentle questions about her time away. Someone joked about whether she had considered extending the sabbatical permanently.

Rachel laughed at the right places. She felt practiced at this, which unsettled her.

When the agenda turned to her sabbatical report, the clerk smiled encouragingly. "No rush," she said. "Just whenever you're ready."

Rachel felt the familiar tightening in her chest. "I'm still working on it," she said. "I want to be thoughtful."

"That makes sense," the clerk replied. "Take the time you need."

Rachel nodded, grateful and trapped all at once.

Later, alone in her office, she reopened the document. The sentences she had left were still there, tentative and incomplete. She read them slowly, as if encountering someone else's words.

I am grateful for the rest, even as I continue to discern its meaning.

She imagined reading it aloud to the session. She imagined the nods, the murmurs of affirmation. She imagined the relief in the room at hearing something that fit the expected shape.

She imagined, too, what she would not be saying.

During sabbatical, she had come to see how often she had absorbed conflict quietly, smoothing edges so that others would not have to feel the discomfort. She had learned to carry the moral tension of decisions she did not make but was responsible for implementing. She had grown adept at translating institutional needs into pastoral language, even when that translation felt like a small betrayal.

None of that had felt optional at the time. It had felt like faithfulness.

Now, rested, she could see the cumulative cost.

Rachel typed a new paragraph, slower this time.

This season of rest has helped me notice the ways I have adapted in order to sustain the work, and the toll those adaptations have taken.

She read it twice. Her pulse quickened. The sentence felt closer to the truth, but it also felt dangerous. Adapted could be read as resilient, which would miss the point entirely. Toll could be acknowledged politely and then set aside.

She added another sentence.

Some of what I am carrying did not originate with me, but has been held quietly over time.

She stopped. The room felt suddenly very still. She imagined the questions that sentence might provoke, the defensiveness it might awaken. She imagined the careful redirection that would follow, the reassurance that no one expected her to carry anything alone.

She laughed softly, a humorless sound.

Rachel deleted the paragraph.

She pushed back from the desk and stood, pacing the small office. Her ordination certificate caught her eye again. She remembered the day it had been handed to her, the way she had felt both exhilarated and sobered by the responsibility it represented. She had not imagined then how much of the work would involve carrying things that could not be named publicly.

That afternoon, she met with a parishioner who wanted to talk about a family conflict. Rachel listened attentively, asked careful questions, offered what support she could. The conversation followed a familiar rhythm, one she knew well. As the parishioner spoke, Rachel felt a strange doubling: she was fully present, and also acutely aware of the irony. She was helping someone name a burden she herself could not yet speak aloud.

After the parishioner left, Rachel sat quietly for a moment, hands folded on the desk. She felt the weight of the day settle into her shoulders.

She opened the letter again.

This time, she did not type. Instead, she stared at the screen and let her mind move freely, unencumbered by the need to be received. She thought of the moments during sabbatical when she had felt a sense of grief surface unexpectedly—on a walk, in the middle of a novel, while washing dishes.

Grief not for something lost suddenly, but for something given slowly and never fully acknowledged.

She thought of the way rest had stripped away her ability to rationalize. How she could no longer tell herself that this was just how ministry was, that everyone felt this way, that the discomfort would pass.

Her phone buzzed again. This time, it was a text from a colleague.

How's the re-entry going? Feeling renewed?

Rachel stared at the message. Her fingers hovered over the screen.

She typed: It's more complicated than I expected.

She hesitated, then hit send.

The reply came quickly.

It usually is. Give it time.

Rachel set the phone down. Time, she thought, was not the issue.

As evening settled in, she finally closed the letter without saving, again. She shut down the computer and turned off the lamp. The office darkened, the familiar shapes softened by shadow.

Before leaving, she took a yellow legal pad from a drawer and wrote a single sentence across the top page.

What if the problem isn't that I'm tired?

She tore the page out and folded it carefully, slipping it into her bag.

Rachel locked the office door behind her and stepped into the quiet hallway. As she walked toward the exit, she felt the familiar pull to make this easier, to find language that would reassure everyone—including herself.

But beneath that impulse was a steadier awareness now, one that sabbatical had made impossible to ignore: whatever she wrote, whatever she said, would have to reckon not with expectations, but with truth.

And truth, she was learning, required more than rest to carry.

The conversation she had been avoiding arrived without warning.

Rachel was standing in the narthex after worship, holding a paper cup of coffee she did not want, when the executive pastor approached her. He smiled easily, the way he always did when he thought things were on track.

"Good to have you back," he said. "Really feels like things are settling."

Rachel nodded. "It's good to be back."

They stood side by side, watching people drift toward the doors. Someone stopped to say hello, another to comment on the sermon. Rachel responded warmly, automatically. When the space around them cleared again, the executive pastor turned slightly toward her.

"I wanted to check in about your sabbatical reflections," he said. "No pressure. Just wanted to make sure you had what you needed."

Rachel felt the familiar tightening, but she kept her voice even. "I'm still working on them."

"Of course," he said. "It's just that the session is eager to hear what the time away has meant for you. Especially in terms of vision."

Vision. The word landed with a dull thud.

"I'm not sure it's that kind of clarity," Rachel said carefully.

He tilted his head, listening. "That's okay too. Sometimes it takes a while for things to integrate."

She nodded. Integration was another safe word. It implied patience without asking questions.

"Well," he said, glancing at his watch, "let me know how I can support you."

"Thank you," Rachel replied.

He smiled again and stepped away, already greeting someone else.

Rachel stood alone for a moment longer, the noise of conversation rising around her. She felt oddly detached from it, as if she were watching the scene through a pane of glass. She finished her coffee and set the cup down, then slipped back into her office and closed the door.

She sat at her desk and stared at the wall. Vision. Integration. Support. The words lined up neatly, offering reassurance without invitation. She wondered how many times she had used them herself, sincerely, with others.

She opened the letter again.

The screen filled with the partial sentences she had left behind, each one an attempt to approach something obliquely. She scrolled slowly, reading as if the words belonged to someone else.

Her fingers hovered over the keyboard.

She began again, this time not editing herself before the words appeared.

During sabbatical, I came to see more clearly the ways I have been carrying unresolved moral tension in this role.

She paused, heart pounding. She added another sentence.

That tension did not arise from overwork or exhaustion, but from prolonged situations where my agency was constrained and my integrity felt divided.

She leaned back, breathing shallowly. The room felt charged now, as if something had been named that could not easily be taken back.

She read the paragraph again, imagining it being read aloud. She could already hear the responses.

We all feel that sometimes.

That's just leadership.

Maybe this is something to explore with a coach.

None of those responses would be cruel. None would be wrong, exactly. All would miss the point.

Rachel highlighted the paragraph and stared at it, finger hovering over the delete key.

She thought of the sabbatical again, of the mornings she had woken without dread, of the way her body had slowly let go of the constant vigilance she had mistaken for devotion. She thought of the grief that had surfaced not because something new had happened, but because she could finally feel what had been there all along.

She did not delete the paragraph.

Instead, she saved the document for the first time.

The relief was brief.

That afternoon, she met with the clerk of session. It was meant to be a routine check-in, a chance to talk about scheduling and re-entry. They sat across from each other at the small conference table, sunlight pooling between them.

"You seem thoughtful," the clerk said kindly. "How are you doing, really?"

Rachel considered the question. She felt the weight of the paragraph she had written pressing against her ribs.

"I'm doing okay," she said. "But I'm also aware that sabbatical didn't solve everything."

The clerk nodded. "It rarely does. Sometimes it just brings things into focus."

Rachel looked at her, surprised. "Yes," she said. "Exactly."

They sat with that for a moment. The clerk smiled gently. "Well, you don't have to have it all figured out. We trust you."

Rachel felt a familiar mix of gratitude and frustration. Trust, she was learning, could be both a gift and a boundary. It allowed space, but it also discouraged disturbance.

"I'm working on a letter," Rachel said. "Trying to be honest."

"That's good," the clerk replied. "Honesty is always appreciated."

Rachel nodded, knowing how elastic that word could be.

When the meeting ended, Rachel returned to her office and closed the door. She opened the letter again and read the paragraph she had saved. It still felt risky. It also felt necessary.

She added one more sentence.

I am still discerning what faithfulness looks like in light of this clarity.

She stopped there. The sentence felt like a bridge she was not yet ready to cross.

As evening approached, Rachel shut down her computer and gathered her things. She slipped the folded page from her bag—the question she had written days earlier—and smoothed it on the desk.

What if the problem isn't that I'm tired?

She added a second line beneath it.

What if the problem is that I can no longer pretend not to know?

She folded the page again and placed it back in her bag.

As she turned off the light and stepped into the hallway, Rachel felt a strange steadiness settle over her. Not the practiced steadiness she had relied on for years, but something quieter, more fragile. The steadiness of someone who had stopped trying to make the truth fit the room.

She knew the letter was not finished. She also knew that whatever shape it eventually took, it would mark a point of no return. Rest had done its work. Clarity had arrived.

Now she would have to decide what to do with it.

And whether there was a place, in this system she loved, where such clarity could be carried without being reshaped into something safer.

The letter began to follow her.

Rachel noticed it first in the small pauses between things, the moments when she would ordinarily let her mind drift. Standing at the sink washing dishes. Waiting at a red light. Sitting through a meeting while someone else spoke at length about something that did not quite matter. The sentences she had written would surface unbidden, their weight pressing in at unexpected times.

She had not sent the letter to anyone. She had not even told herself, honestly, who it was for.

The session meeting loomed on the calendar, its date circled lightly in pencil. Rachel found herself counting backward from it, measuring how much time she had left before the letter would need to exist in some form other than draft. She told herself she could still revise it, soften it, make it more pastoral, more digestible. She told herself many things.

On a Tuesday afternoon, she met with her spiritual director, a woman she had been seeing for years. The office was small and spare, with two chairs angled toward each other and a low table between them. A candle burned quietly in the corner.

Rachel settled into her chair and let out a long breath.

"You look steadier," her director said, after a moment.

Rachel smiled faintly. "I don't feel steadier. I feel. . . clearer."

The director nodded. "Sometimes clarity feels like that."

Rachel hesitated, then reached into her bag and pulled out a folded sheet of paper. She smoothed it on her lap, then handed it across the small space between them.

"I wrote something," she said. "It's not finished."

The director took the paper without comment and read silently. Rachel watched her face, alert for any sign of alarm or confusion. None came. When she finished, the director folded the paper carefully and held it for a moment.

"What do you want this letter to do?" she asked gently.

Rachel swallowed. "I don't know," she said. "I want it to tell the truth. But I don't want it to cause harm."

The director nodded slowly. "Those are not always compatible goals."

Rachel felt the truth of that settle in her chest.

"I keep thinking there must be a way to say this that will land well," Rachel continued. "A way to make it constructive."

"And what happens if it doesn't?" the director asked.

Rachel was quiet for a long moment. She felt the familiar urge to manage the question, to find the response that would demonstrate maturity and restraint. She let the urge pass.

"Then I'll know," she said finally, "that the problem isn't how I'm saying it."

The director met her gaze. "And what would that mean?"

Rachel's voice was barely above a whisper. "That there may not be room here for what I now know."

They sat in silence, the candle flickering softly.

When Rachel returned to her office afterward, she closed the door and opened the letter again. She read it from beginning to end without stopping. The words felt less volatile now, though no less true. She noticed where she had hedged, where she had tried to anticipate the reader's discomfort. She began to revise—not to soften, but to clarify.

She removed a paragraph that explained too much. She replaced it with one sentence.

What sabbatical revealed was not fatigue, but moral strain accumulated over time.

She paused, then added another.

I can no longer unsee this.

The simplicity of the sentences startled her. She read them again, letting them stand without defense.

Later that week, she met with the executive pastor again, this time by appointment. They sat across from each other in his office, the same neutral artwork on the walls, the same careful order to the space.

"I wanted to share where I am," Rachel said, surprising herself with how calm she felt.

He leaned forward slightly. "Of course."

She spoke slowly, choosing words that were precise rather than reassuring. She named the clarity sabbatical had brought, the way rest had revealed rather than resolved the strain she had been carrying. She did not use the language of burnout. She did not apologize.

He listened without interrupting. When she finished, he nodded thoughtfully.

"That sounds heavy," he said. "Have you considered extending your time with a coach? Or perhaps another short leave?"

Rachel felt a familiar disappointment, but it did not sting as sharply as she had expected.

"I don't think more time away will change what I now understand," she said. "This isn't about capacity. It's about alignment."

He frowned slightly, then smiled. "Sometimes alignment takes time."

"Yes," Rachel agreed. "But sometimes it requires change."

The conversation ended politely, without resolution. As Rachel left the office, she felt neither defeated nor relieved. She felt informed.

The night before the session meeting, Rachel sat at her desk and read the letter one final time. She imagined the faces of the people who would receive it, their care, their concern, their limits. She imagined the room holding her words, reshaping them gently, returning them altered.

She folded the letter and placed it in an envelope. She did not address it yet.

Outside, the neighborhood was quiet. The maple tree by the window was bare now, its branches etched against the dark sky. Rachel rested her hands on the desk and breathed.

She knew that sending the letter would not solve anything. It would not guarantee understanding or change. But it would mark a boundary she could no longer cross back over.

Rest had given her clarity. Clarity had given her responsibility.

Rachel turned off the lamp and stood. The letter lay on the desk, sealed but not yet sent. She did not know what the meeting would bring. She did not know how her words would be received.

She only knew that bearing this alone was no longer an option.

Whatever came next would require the truth to exist somewhere beyond her own careful keeping.

And tomorrow, she would decide whether the room was ready—or whether she would need to find another place to set this weight down.

The session meeting began the way they always did, with coffee poured too quickly and chairs scraping against the floor as people settled into familiar places. Rachel arrived early, the envelope tucked carefully into her bag, its weight disproportionate to its size. She greeted people as they arrived, smiling, making space, answering questions about schedules and logistics. No one mentioned the letter. No one yet knew it existed.

The opening prayer was offered by the clerk, measured and sincere. Rachel bowed her head and listened, noting the words chosen: gratitude, guidance, patience. She wondered, briefly, what patience meant when clarity had already arrived.

The agenda moved steadily. Reports were given. Decisions were deferred. Rachel participated as expected, her voice steady, her contributions thoughtful and contained. She could feel the envelope in her bag like a quiet pulse.

When they reached the sabbatical report, the clerk glanced toward her. "Rachel," she said warmly, "whenever you're ready."

Rachel took a breath. She felt the familiar urge to preface, to soften what she was about to do. She resisted it.

"I've prepared something," she said. "It's a written reflection."

She reached into her bag and placed the envelope on the table in front of her. The simple gesture felt momentous, as if she were setting down something that had been held too tightly for too long.

"I want to name up front," she continued, "that this isn't a report about productivity or outcomes. It's an attempt to speak honestly about what sabbatical revealed."

The room was very still. Rachel could feel attention sharpen, curiosity mingled with unease.

She opened the envelope and took out the letter. Her hands did not shake.

She read slowly, allowing the words to land without embellishment. She spoke of rest and clarity, of the ways sabbatical had quieted her body enough for long-held moral strain to become visible. She named the difference between exhaustion and misalignment, between capacity and integrity. She did not accuse. She did not apologize.

When she finished, she folded the letter and placed it back in the envelope.

For a moment, no one spoke.

Then the clerk smiled gently. "Thank you for sharing that," she said. "It took courage."

Others nodded. Someone murmured assent. Rachel waited, aware that affirmation was often the easiest response.

A session member leaned forward. "I'm wondering," he said carefully, "whether some of what you're describing might ease with time. Re-entry can be disorienting."

Another added, "Yes, sometimes after sabbatical there's a letdown. It doesn't mean something's wrong."

Rachel listened. She felt the familiar pattern forming, the collective instinct to normalize and reassure. She had anticipated this. It still stung.

"I hear that," she said evenly. "And I've considered it. What I'm trying to say is that this feels different. It's not about adjustment. It's about knowing something I can't unknow."

The room shifted slightly. The chair cleared her throat. "Can you say more about what you mean by misalignment?"

Rachel paused. She considered the question, the way it invited elaboration while narrowing the frame. She chose her response carefully.

"I mean that I've become more aware of the cost of certain patterns we've accepted as necessary," she said. "And I'm not sure I can continue to absorb that cost quietly."

Silence returned, heavier now.

The executive pastor spoke. "We care deeply about you," he said. "And we want to support you. Perhaps we could explore some additional resources—coaching, maybe a phased return?"

Rachel nodded. "I appreciate that. I'm open to support. What I'm asking is whether we can also consider what might need to change beyond me."

The question hung in the air.

The chair glanced around the table. "That's a larger conversation," she said finally. "One we may not be able to resolve tonight."

Rachel felt a familiar mix of disappointment and relief. She had not expected resolution. She had expected recognition.

"I understand," she said. "I just needed to bring it into the room."

The meeting moved on.

After adjournment, people lingered longer than usual. Several approached Rachel, thanking her, telling her they admired her honesty. Their words were kind, sincere. She accepted them graciously, aware of the limits of such exchanges.

As she gathered her things, the clerk came over. "I'm glad you spoke," she said quietly. "Even if we're not sure what to do yet."

Rachel smiled. "So am I."

Outside, the evening air was cool. Rachel stood on the steps for a moment, breathing deeply. She felt lighter, though not relieved. The weight had shifted, redistributed, but not disappeared.

She walked to her car and sat behind the wheel without starting the engine. She thought of the letter, now shared, its words no longer hers alone. She thought of the room, its care, its caution.

She also thought of the spiritual director's question: What do you want this letter to do?

Rachel did not have a full answer yet. But she knew one thing clearly: the letter had done what it needed to do today. It had told the truth without shrinking.

As she drove home, the streetlights flickered on one by one, illuminating the road ahead in small, steady increments. Rachel followed them, aware that whatever came next would require continued attention, continued courage.

She was no longer carrying this alone.

And that, she realized, was a beginning—even if it was not the ending anyone had expected.

The days after the session meeting unfolded quietly.

Rachel had expected something sharper—a backlash, perhaps, or an urgent flurry of follow-up meetings. Instead, there was a gentle deceleration, as if the system were absorbing what had been said without yet knowing how to respond. Emails arrived that thanked her again for her honesty. A few suggested next steps without specifying them. Most said nothing at all.

She returned to her routines, preaching on Sunday, visiting a parishioner in the hospital, meeting with a couple preparing for marriage. The work itself had not changed. What had changed was her relationship to it. She noticed now how often she had once overridden her own hesitation, how quickly she had translated discomfort into accommodation. She felt less able to do that now, and less willing.

One afternoon, she received a message from the executive pastor asking if she had time to talk. They met later that week, sitting across from each other with mugs of coffee growing cold between them.

"I've been thinking about what you shared," he said. "And about the conversation it opened."

Rachel nodded, listening.

"There's concern," he continued carefully. "Not about your integrity, but about sustainability. About what it means if leaders feel they can't stay when things are hard."

Rachel felt the familiar tightening, but she did not interrupt.

"I understand that concern," she said when he finished. "What I'm naming isn't about avoiding difficulty. It's about not absorbing moral strain indefinitely without acknowledgment or shared responsibility."

He leaned back, considering this. "That may be true," he said. "But systems move slowly."

"Yes," Rachel replied. "And people don't."

The conversation ended politely, without resolution. As she left the office, Rachel felt neither dismissed nor reassured. She felt something else: informed. The contours of what was possible were becoming clearer, even if the path forward was not.

That night, she returned home later than usual. The house was quiet, the lights low. She set her bag down and sat at the kitchen table without turning on the overhead light. The letter—now a shared artifact—no longer sat on her desk. She felt its absence like a phantom weight.

She thought of the sabbatical again, of the long walks and unstructured days. She realized that rest had not prepared her to stay in the same way. It had prepared her to see.

A week later, the clerk of session stopped by her office. She stood in the doorway, hands folded loosely.

"I wanted you to know," she said, "that your letter is still with us. We're talking about it."

Rachel smiled faintly. "I hoped it would be."

The clerk hesitated. "I don't know what that will mean yet."

Rachel met her gaze. "Neither do I."

After she left, Rachel sat quietly, feeling the truth of that exchange settle. The letter had done what it could. It had named something real. What happened next would depend on whether the system could bear it.

As spring deepened, Rachel noticed small changes in herself. She spoke more slowly in meetings, leaving space where she might once have rushed to fill it. She declined one request that would have stretched her thin, offering a clear explanation without apology. She felt exposed at first, then steadier.

One evening, as she prepared a sermon, she paused over a line in the text about truth setting people free. She smiled at the familiarity of the phrase, then felt its weight anew. Freedom, she was learning, was not relief. It was responsibility.

The following month, she met again with her spiritual director.

"How does it feel now?" the director asked.

Rachel considered the question. "Unfinished," she said. "But honest."

The director nodded. "That's often where faithfulness lives."

On her way home, Rachel stopped at a park she had walked through often during sabbatical. The trees were full now, the grass thick and green. She sat on a bench and watched children play nearby, their laughter carrying easily in the warm air.

She thought of the question she had written weeks earlier: What if the problem isn't that I'm tired?

She knew the answer now. The problem had never been exhaustion. It had been silence.

Rachel stood and walked slowly back to her car. She did not know whether she would remain in this role long-term. She did not know whether the institution could change in ways that would make staying possible. What she knew was simpler and harder: she could no longer pretend not to know what she knew.

As she drove away, the light fading behind her, Rachel felt the weight she carried settle into a different shape. It was still heavy. It still mattered.

But it was no longer hidden.

And for now, that was enough to bear.

STORY 3

"What We Mean by Process"

The first thing Linda noticed was how carefully everything was named.

Not the conflict itself—that remained vaguely described, its edges softened by language that suggested complexity rather than harm. What was named precisely were the steps: intake, review, consultation, response. Each stage had a title, a timeline, a document attached. The words lay on the page in orderly rows, reassuring in their symmetry.

Linda had been on the committee long enough to recognize the comfort this brought. Process gave shape to uncertainty. It allowed people to move forward without appearing to rush, to act without appearing reactive. It was, she had once believed, a form of faithfulness.

She arrived at the meeting early, as she usually did, and took her place near the middle of the table. The room was smaller than the one used for larger gatherings, with windows that looked out over a courtyard no one ever used. A stack of binders sat at the center, each labeled identically, the conflict reduced to a single, neutral phrase.

She opened her binder and scanned the contents. Familiar headings greeted her. Background. Timeline. Current status. Linda felt the faint sense of relief that came with knowing where things were supposed to go, even if she was less certain about where they were actually heading.

Others filtered in, greeting one another quietly. There was a shared understanding among them, unspoken but firm: this was serious work. They were careful people, committed people. They had been chosen because they could be trusted not to make things worse.

The chair called the meeting to order. The opening prayer asked for wisdom and patience. Linda bowed her head, listening. Patience had become the virtue most often invoked in this room. She wondered, not for the first time, what it cost.

They began with a review of the timeline. Dates were read aloud, each one marking a step taken, a conversation held, a response issued. Linda followed along, pen in hand, though she rarely wrote anything down anymore. The rhythm of these meetings had become predictable, almost soothing.

As the chair spoke, Linda found herself thinking of the pastor at the center of it all. She had met him only once, briefly, in a hallway after an earlier meeting. He had smiled politely, thanked her for her service. His eyes had lingered just long enough to suggest he wanted to say something else, then he had nodded and walked away.

Linda had told herself at the time that distance was appropriate. Boundaries mattered. This was not personal.

The update continued. Consultants had been engaged. Additional information gathered. No new action recommended at this time.

Linda felt a familiar tightening in her chest. She glanced around the table. Everyone was attentive, serious, composed. No one looked surprised.

She raised her hand.

"Yes, Linda?" the chair said.

"I'm wondering," Linda began, choosing her words with care, "how we're considering the impact of this timeline on the pastor involved."

The chair nodded. "That's an important question. And it's something we're mindful of."

Linda waited.

"We don't want to rush the process," another member added. "Rushing can create more harm."

"Of course," Linda said. She meant it. She also felt the inadequacy of the response settle in her body.

They moved on.

As the meeting progressed, Linda felt herself slipping into observation rather than participation. She listened closely to the language being used, the way responsibility was distributed across the group without ever quite landing anywhere. Phrases like we need to be careful and it's complicated circulated freely, offering protection without direction.

At one point, someone referred to the pastor's situation as unfortunate. Linda flinched inwardly. The word carried a sense of inevitability, as if the outcome were a matter of bad luck rather than a series of decisions.

She thought again of the hallway encounter, the pastor's eyes. She wondered how long he had been waiting, how many times he had been told that the process was ongoing, that clarity would come.

The meeting adjourned on schedule. Chairs scraped, binders were closed. People gathered their things with the quiet efficiency of those accustomed to leaving difficult matters unresolved.

As Linda stood, the chair touched her arm briefly. "Thank you for your question," she said. "It's good to keep those concerns in view."

Linda smiled. "I'm glad to help."

The words came easily. Too easily.

In the hallway, she paused, watching as others dispersed. The building felt hushed, the way it always did after meetings like this. She wondered where the pastor was now—whether he was preparing a sermon, visiting a parishioner, trying not to think about this room and the careful words spoken inside it.

Linda walked toward the exit, her steps slower than usual. She felt a growing awareness, not yet a conviction, that something in this process was misaligned. Everything was being done correctly. And yet, something essential was being missed.

Outside, the air was cool and bright. Linda stood for a moment, breathing deeply. She told herself that patience mattered, that fairness required time. She told herself that process existed to protect everyone involved.

Still, as she walked to her car, she could not shake the sense that the protection was unevenly distributed.

Somewhere along the way, she thought, process had become something else entirely.

And she was no longer certain she knew what it was meant to protect.

Linda noticed the shift the next morning, though she could not have named it if asked.

It was not dramatic. Nothing in her schedule had changed. The committee meeting already felt slightly distant, filed away under ongoing matters. And yet, as she sat at her desk reviewing emails, she found herself rereading phrases she had skimmed past for years.

Pending further review.

Out of an abundance of caution.

In accordance with established procedure.

They appeared everywhere, familiar and unremarkable. Linda had used them herself countless times. Now they seemed oddly loud.

She closed her laptop and leaned back in her chair. Through the window, she could see the courtyard below, its benches empty, the landscaping carefully maintained. She wondered who the space was meant for. No one ever lingered there. It existed, like much of the system she served, as a symbol of care more than a site of it.

Her phone buzzed. A message from the chair.

Thanks again for yesterday. Helpful questions.

Linda stared at the screen. The phrase settled uneasily in her chest. Helpful. She typed a response, erased it, then sent a simple acknowledgment. She did not know what else to say.

Later that afternoon, she met with a colleague from another committee. They talked about budgets, about staffing concerns, about how tired everyone seemed lately.

"It's just one thing after another," her colleague said, rubbing her temples. "I'm so glad we have good process. At least that keeps things from blowing up."

Linda nodded automatically. Then she hesitated.

"Do you ever worry," she asked slowly, "that process sometimes keeps things from being addressed at all?"

Her colleague laughed lightly. "I think I know what you mean. But honestly, without it, things would get messy fast."

Linda smiled, the conversation already moving on. Still, the question lingered.

That evening, Linda found herself thinking again about the pastor. She realized she did not actually know how long the situation had been ongoing. Months, certainly. Possibly longer. The timeline in the binder was precise but oddly abstract, each entry stripped of context.

She pulled the binder from her bag and laid it on the kitchen table. Opening it felt slightly transgressive, as if she were revisiting something meant to stay contained in the meeting room.

She flipped through the pages slowly, reading not just the content but the shape of it. The way concerns were introduced, the way they were reframed, the way responsibility drifted upward and outward until it dissolved.

Linda stopped at a section labeled Current Status. The language was careful, almost soothing.

No immediate action required at this time.

She felt a flicker of irritation. Immediate, she thought, for whom?

She closed the binder and sat back, folding her hands in her lap. The question that had been forming since the meeting finally surfaced clearly: What was process doing here, exactly?

She had always believed it existed to protect the vulnerable—to ensure fairness, to prevent rash decisions, to slow things down when emotions ran high. All of that was still true. But she was beginning to see another function, one she had not wanted to acknowledge.

Process also protected those who administered it.

It allowed harm to be described without being felt. It converted urgency into manageability. It gave everyone something to point to when asked why nothing had changed.

Linda thought of the chair's reassurance: We're mindful of that. She wondered what mindfulness meant when it never translated into movement.

The next committee meeting came sooner than she expected. As she drove to the building, Linda felt a low-grade tension she could not quite place. She told herself it was simply the gravity of the work. She told herself she was overthinking things.

The meeting followed a familiar pattern. Updates were given. Consultants referenced. The same phrases surfaced again, unchanged. Linda listened carefully, her attention sharpened by the questions she had not yet asked.

At one point, someone suggested extending the timeline to allow for additional review. Heads nodded. No one objected.

Linda felt her hand lift before she had fully decided to speak.

"I want to make sure I understand," she said, her voice steady. "What does extending the timeline change for the pastor involved?"

The room grew still.

The chair responded smoothly. "It allows us to be thorough. To avoid unintended consequences."

"Yes," Linda said. "And what are the consequences of waiting?"

The question hung in the air. Linda could feel the room recalibrating, the familiar discomfort settling in.

Another member spoke. "We don't want to speculate."

"I'm not asking us to speculate," Linda replied. "I'm asking us to acknowledge what we already know."

The chair folded her hands. "Linda, we need to be careful not to step outside our role."

Linda nodded. She recognized the boundary being drawn, the gentle reminder of how things were done here.

"I understand," she said. And she did. That was part of the problem.

The meeting moved on, but something had shifted. Linda could feel it in herself, if not in the room. She had crossed a small internal line, one that made it harder to retreat into comfortable abstraction.

After adjournment, she lingered behind, gathering her things slowly. The chair approached her again, her expression kind but measured.

"I appreciate your concern," she said. "Truly. Just remember, we're accountable to the process."

Linda met her gaze. "I know."

What she did not say was that she was beginning to wonder who the process was accountable to.

Outside, the afternoon sun was bright, almost cheerful. Linda stood for a moment, feeling its warmth on her face. She thought of the courtyard, of the empty benches. She thought of the pastor, still waiting.

She realized then that the discomfort she felt was not doubt about the process itself. It was doubt about her own participation in it.

Process, she was learning, did not absolve responsibility. It redistributed it.

And the longer she remained silent, the more clearly she could see where her share of it lay.

Linda began to notice how often people invoked process as if it were a place.

Not a method, not a sequence of actions, but somewhere you could stand when things became uncomfortable. We're in process. Let's stay in process. Trust the process. The phrases appeared in emails and conversations, offering a kind of shelter. They allowed people to pause without appearing inactive, to defer without appearing avoidant.

She had said them herself. Often.

The realization unsettled her more than outright disagreement would have.

A week after the last meeting, Linda received a packet in her inbox. An updated summary, neatly formatted, the language smoothed further. She read it once, then again more slowly. The pastor's situation was described as ongoing, the concerns complex, the next steps under consideration.

Nothing in the document was inaccurate. That was the problem.

She forwarded it to a colleague on the committee, adding a brief note: Would you be open to talking about this before the next meeting?

The reply came an hour later. Happy to. I've been feeling uneasy too.

They met over lunch at a quiet café near the building. Linda arrived early and chose a table by the window. When her colleague, Marsha, joined her, Linda noticed the same tension in her posture that she felt in herself—a kind of alertness that came from knowing something mattered but not yet knowing what to do with that knowledge.

"I'm glad you reached out," Marsha said after they ordered. "I thought it was just me."

Linda nodded. "I don't think it is."

They sat in silence for a moment, the low hum of conversation around them filling the space.

"I keep telling myself we're being careful," Marsha said finally. "That we're protecting everyone involved. But I don't know who everyone is anymore."

Linda felt a small release at hearing her own thoughts spoken aloud. "That's exactly it," she said. "Careful for whom?"

Marsha frowned slightly. "If we act too quickly, we risk getting it wrong."

"And if we don't act," Linda replied, "we risk something else."

Marsha nodded. "The pastor."

They let the word sit between them.

"I think what bothers me," Marsha continued, "is that the longer this goes on, the less agency he seems to have. And we call that fairness."

Linda felt the truth of it settle heavily. "We keep saying we're neutral," she said. "But neutrality still lands somewhere."

Their food arrived. They ate slowly, the conversation ebbing and flowing. They did not arrive at solutions. They did not plan a strategy. What they did instead was acknowledge, quietly and honestly, that something was wrong.

As they stood to leave, Marsha hesitated. "Be careful," she said. "You know how this can be read."

Linda smiled faintly. "I do."

The warning was not unkind. It was practical.

At the next committee meeting, Linda came prepared. Not with a speech, but with a decision she had already made. She would no longer hide behind abstraction.

When the agenda reached the familiar item, the chair summarized the update, her tone steady. Linda listened, then raised her hand.

"Yes, Linda?" the chair said.

"I want to ask a different kind of question," Linda said. Her voice sounded calm, though she felt her pulse quicken. "What would it look like to center the pastor's moral safety in this process?"

The room went very still.

The chair blinked. "Can you clarify what you mean by that?"

"Yes," Linda said. "We talk a lot about risk and fairness. I'm asking how we are ensuring that the person most affected by this isn't being asked to endure harm simply because we are moving slowly."

Someone shifted in their chair. Another glanced down at their notes.

"That's a strong framing," a member said cautiously.

"I know," Linda replied. "But I think it's an accurate one."

The chair folded her hands. "Our role isn't to evaluate moral experience," she said. "It's to follow the established process."

Linda felt the familiar boundary snap into place, clear and firm.

"I understand our role," she said. "I'm asking whether the process is doing what we believe it's doing."

Silence.

Then Marsha spoke. "I think Linda's pointing to something important," she said. "We keep extending timelines in the name of caution, but we haven't named the cost of that extension."

The chair looked around the table. "We need to be careful not to personalize this," she said.

Linda nodded. "I'm not trying to personalize it. I'm trying to humanize it."

The distinction felt crucial.

The conversation that followed was tense but restrained. No one raised their voice. No one accused. And yet, something fundamental had been disturbed. Linda could feel it in the way people spoke more slowly, more deliberately, as if choosing each word required new effort.

In the end, the chair proposed forming a subcommittee to explore the concerns raised. The suggestion was met with relief. It offered movement without commitment, attention without action.

Linda agreed to serve on it.

After the meeting, as people gathered their things, the chair approached her. "I hope you know," she said, "that I respect your commitment. But this kind of language can make people defensive."

Linda met her gaze. "I'm less worried about defensiveness than I am about silence."

The chair studied her for a moment, then nodded. "I hear you."

Linda wasn't sure that was true. But it was closer than she had been before.

That evening, at home, Linda sat at her kitchen table with the binder open in front of her. She flipped through the pages again, this time imagining how they would read to someone outside the room. Someone who did not know the shorthand, the intentions, the careful balancing acts.

They would read as thorough. As fair. As patient.

They would not read as what Linda was beginning to understand them to be: a record of avoidance that no one had intended.

She closed the binder and leaned back, feeling the weight of the day settle into her shoulders. She knew that speaking this way would not make her popular. She knew it could be interpreted as impatience, or worse, as disloyalty.

She also knew that returning to the comfort of process-as-shelter was no longer possible.

Once you saw how neutrality could wound, you could not unsee it.

Linda stood and turned off the light. The house grew quiet around her. As she headed for bed, she felt a mix of resolve and grief. Resolve to keep asking the questions she now knew mattered. Grief for the simplicity she had lost.

Process, she was learning, was not wrong.

But it was not innocent.

And now that she understood that, she would have to decide how much of herself she was willing to risk to say so.

The subcommittee met on a Tuesday morning, three people seated around a smaller table than usual, as if proximity itself might force something more honest. Linda arrived early, again, and placed her binder in front of her without opening it. She had read it enough. She did not need its reassurance today.

Marsha arrived next, offering a tight smile. "This feels. . . significant," she said, settling into her chair.

"It does," Linda replied. "Though I'm not sure the task will be allowed to be."

The third member, James, arrived a few minutes later. He was thoughtful, methodical, respected for his ability to keep discussions grounded. Linda had always trusted his judgment. She wondered, now, how far that trust could stretch.

The chair of the full committee had framed their charge carefully: to explore concerns raised about the experience of the pastor within the current process and report back with recommendations.

Explore. Report. Recommend.

They began, as expected, by reviewing documents. James summarized the timeline again, his voice steady. Marsha nodded along, adding clarifications where needed. Linda listened, her attention drifting not to what was said, but to what was avoided.

At one point, James looked up. "I think it's important to acknowledge," he said, "that everything we've done so far aligns with policy."

Linda felt the familiar pull toward agreement. She let it pass.

"Yes," she said instead. "And I think it's equally important to acknowledge that alignment with policy hasn't prevented harm."

James frowned slightly. "Harm is a strong word."

"It is," Linda agreed. "But I think it's accurate."

Marsha leaned forward. "What do we mean by harm, exactly?" she asked.

Linda took a breath. "I mean prolonged moral strain. Being required to remain in an unresolved situation without meaningful agency, while decisions are deferred elsewhere."

James was quiet for a moment. "We can't base decisions on subjective experience alone," he said carefully.

Linda nodded. "I'm not suggesting we do. I'm suggesting we recognize that subjective experience doesn't become irrelevant just because it's difficult to measure."

The room fell silent. Linda could feel the tension, the careful calibration each of them was performing internally. This was the edge of what the subcommittee was permitted to do.

Marsha broke the silence. "What if we named the cost of the timeline explicitly?" she suggested. "Not to assign blame, but to make it visible."

James considered this. "That might be interpreted as criticism of the committee."

"Or as honesty," Linda said.

He smiled faintly. "Those aren't always distinguished."

They worked for over an hour, circling the same questions from different angles. Each attempt to move toward clarity encountered the same invisible boundary. They could describe. They could contextualize. They could not conclude.

In the end, they drafted a recommendation that suggested increased pastoral support for the individual involved and a commitment to revisiting timelines regularly. The language was careful, almost elegant.

Linda read it twice, feeling the familiar disappointment settle in.

"It's not wrong," she said slowly. "But it's not enough."

James looked at her, his expression kind but weary. "We can only recommend what the system can receive."

The sentence landed heavily.

Linda realized then that this was the crux of it. Not whether the process was flawed, but whether it could bear the truth of its own limits.

The subcommittee disbanded, their work complete. Linda returned to her car and sat for a moment before starting the engine. She felt the familiar mix of resolve and grief again, sharper now.

That evening, her phone rang. The pastor's name appeared on the screen.

She hesitated, then answered.

"Linda," he said. "I hope this is okay."

"Of course," she replied. "I'm glad you called."

They spoke carefully at first, both aware of the boundaries that technically existed. He thanked her for her service, for her questions. He said he knew things took time.

"I wanted to tell you," he said finally, "that I'm not sure how much longer I can do this."

Linda closed her eyes. "I hear that."

"I don't want to make things harder," he continued. "I just needed someone to know."

Linda felt the weight of his words settle into her chest. This was what the binder could not hold. This was what process could not absorb without consequence.

"I'm glad you told me," she said. "You shouldn't be carrying this alone."

There was a pause on the line. "It feels like I already am," he said quietly.

After they hung up, Linda sat in the darkened living room, her phone resting on the table beside her. She felt the accumulated weight of the day press in, heavier than usual. She thought of the subcommittee's recommendation, of its careful insufficiency.

She also thought of her own role. How easy it would be to tell herself she had done what she could. How tempting it would be to retreat into the shelter of process now that she had tested its limits.

But something had shifted. She could not return to innocence.

The next full committee meeting arrived with little fanfare. The subcommittee report was presented, its language received with nods of approval. The chair thanked them for their diligence.

Linda listened, then raised her hand.

"Yes, Linda?" the chair said.

"I want to add something," Linda said, her voice steady. "Not to the report, but to the record."

The room grew still.

"I think we need to acknowledge that while our process is functioning as designed, it is not functioning without cost. And that cost is being borne unevenly."

A pause.

"I don't know what the right next step is," she continued. "But I don't think we can continue without naming that plainly."

The chair looked at her for a long moment. Then she nodded. "That's noted."

The meeting moved on.

Afterward, as Linda gathered her things, Marsha touched her arm. "That took courage," she said.

Linda smiled faintly. "It took clarity."

Outside, the air was crisp. Linda stood for a moment, breathing deeply. She knew that nothing had changed yet. The pastor was still waiting. The system still moved at its careful pace.

But something had been placed on the record.

Process, she now understood, could not save them from moral responsibility. It could only delay its reckoning.

As she walked to her car, Linda felt the weight of that truth settle into her, heavy but unmistakable.

She would have to decide, sooner rather than later, how much more she was willing to carry in the name of being careful.

And whether care, at some point, required something braver than process alone.

Linda slept poorly the night after the meeting.

Not because of anxiety exactly, but because her mind refused to settle. Each time she drifted toward sleep, a phrase from the day resurfaced, insistent and unresolved. Functioning as designed. Uneven cost. Noted.

She rose early, the sky still dim, and made coffee she barely tasted. Sitting at the kitchen table, she opened her notebook—not the binder, not the official documents, but the one she used for thoughts she had no intention of sharing. She stared at the blank page for a long moment, then began to write.

What does it mean to serve a process that cannot hear its own consequences?

The question startled her with its clarity. She wrote it again, slower this time, then set the pen down.

At work later that morning, Linda moved through her responsibilities with practiced competence. Emails were answered. Calls returned. She participated in a meeting unrelated to the committee's work, nodding along as decisions were made efficiently and without controversy. She noticed, with a kind of quiet irony, how satisfying it felt when things moved cleanly.

That afternoon, an email arrived from the chair.

I wanted to follow up on your comments yesterday. I hear your concern, and I want to assure you we are taking it seriously. At the same time, it's important we remain unified in our approach.

Linda read the message twice.

Unified.

She typed a response, erased it, then typed again.

Thank you for reaching out. I appreciate the commitment to care and unity. I also believe unity is strongest when it can hold honest difference.

She hesitated, then sent it.

The reply came an hour later.

Of course. We just need to be mindful of how things are perceived.

Linda closed her laptop and leaned back in her chair. Perception, she thought, had become the quiet arbiter of morality. Not what was true, not what was harmful, but what could be seen without discomfort.

That evening, Linda received another call from the pastor.

"I wanted to let you know," he said, "that I've been asked to be patient again."

Linda closed her eyes. "I'm sorry."

"I know no one is trying to hurt me," he continued. "That's almost the hardest part."

"Yes," Linda said quietly. "It often is."

There was a pause. "I don't want to be disloyal," he said. "But I'm starting to feel erased."

The word lodged in Linda's chest.

"You're not invisible," she said. "Even if it feels that way."

"I appreciate you saying that," he replied. "I just wish it counted for more."

After they hung up, Linda sat in silence, the room darkening around her. She thought of the courtyard again, the unused benches. She thought of the binder, the careful language, the timelines that stretched forward without end.

She also thought of her own limits.

At the next committee meeting, Linda arrived with a different posture. She did not feel urgent. She felt resolved.

When the agenda reached the familiar item, the chair summarized the update with the same careful tone as before. Linda listened, then raised her hand.

"Yes, Linda?" the chair said.

"I want to name something plainly," Linda said. Her voice was calm, but there was no mistaking its seriousness. "I no longer believe that extending this process without decisive action is neutral. It is a decision. And it has consequences."

The room was silent.

"We need to be careful with language like that," someone said.

"I am being careful," Linda replied. "Careful not to confuse procedure with innocence."

The chair's expression tightened. "Linda, are you suggesting we've acted wrongly?"

"I'm suggesting," Linda said, "that we are participating in harm even as we follow the rules."

The words hung in the air, heavy and undeniable.

The chair leaned back, folding her arms. "That's a serious accusation."

"It's a serious situation," Linda said. "And treating it gently hasn't made it less so."

No one spoke for a long moment.

Finally, the chair said, "We'll need to take that under advisement."

Linda nodded. "I expected that."

The meeting moved on, but the atmosphere had changed. People spoke more cautiously now, glancing toward Linda as if recalibrating their understanding of her role. She felt oddly calm.

After adjournment, Marsha caught up with her in the hallway.

"You just crossed a line," she said softly.

"I know," Linda replied.

"Are you okay with that?"

Linda considered the question. "I don't think I could keep pretending the line wasn't there."

Marsha nodded slowly. "I'm glad you said what you did."

Outside, the air was sharp with the promise of rain. Linda stood on the steps, breathing deeply. She felt exposed, but also strangely intact.

She knew what would likely follow. Conversations about tone. About teamwork. About whether this was the right forum for such concerns. She might be asked to step back, or at least to soften.

She also knew that stepping back into silence would now feel like a form of violence—done not to others, but to herself.

That night, Linda returned to her notebook and wrote again.

Process can slow harm. It can also conceal it.

She closed the notebook and sat quietly, letting the truth of that sentence settle. She did not know how this would end. She did not know whether the system could change, or whether she would need to change her relationship to it.

What she knew was this: once the moral cost of process became visible, continuing without protest was no longer a neutral act.

Linda turned off the light and went to bed, aware that whatever sleep came would be lighter now, edged with clarity.

The work of naming had begun.

And naming, she was learning, always carried its own weight.

The request came a week later.

Linda was finishing lunch at her desk when the email arrived from the chair, brief and carefully worded.

Could we talk?

There was no subject line. No urgency marker. Just the quiet gravity of a conversation that had already been partially decided.

They met that afternoon in the same conference room where so many careful sentences had been spoken. The table was cleared now, no binders, no placards. The absence of materials felt intentional, as if the conversation were meant to be personal rather than procedural.

The chair gestured for Linda to sit. She did.

"I want to start by saying how much we value your service," the chair began. "Your commitment. Your integrity."

Linda nodded. She had learned to listen closely when compliments came first.

"At the same time," the chair continued, "there's concern about how some of your recent comments have landed."

Linda folded her hands in her lap. "I imagined there might be."

"It's not that the concerns themselves are illegitimate," the chair said. "It's the way they're being framed. Language about harm and complicity—it can feel accusatory."

Linda took a breath. She felt tired, but not defensive.

"I'm trying to be accurate," she said. "Not accusatory."

"I understand that," the chair replied. "But this committee relies on trust. On people believing we're acting in good faith."

Linda met her gaze. "I do believe that. Acting in good faith doesn't mean acting without consequence."

The chair sighed, a sound of genuine weariness. "Linda, we're all doing the best we can within the constraints we have."

"I know," Linda said. "That's part of what I'm naming."

There was a pause. The chair glanced toward the window, then back at Linda.

"We're wondering," she said carefully, "whether it might be helpful for you to step back from this particular case."

The words landed with surprising gentleness.

Linda absorbed them slowly. She had expected something like this. Still, the finality of it caught in her chest.

"You mean recuse myself," she said.

"Yes," the chair replied. "Not as a punishment. As a way to protect the integrity of the process—and you."

Linda almost smiled at that. Protection had become such a flexible word.

"I appreciate the concern," she said. "But stepping back doesn't resolve what I'm seeing. It just removes me from having to witness it."

The chair's expression tightened slightly. "Sometimes witnessing from a distance is healthier."

"For whom?" Linda asked.

The question hung between them.

After a moment, the chair said, "We'll give you some time to think about it."

Linda nodded. "Thank you."

When she left the room, Linda felt oddly calm. The hallway looked the same as it always did, the carpet worn smooth by years of careful walking. She moved through it slowly, aware that something fundamental had shifted.

That evening, she called Marsha.

"They asked me to step back," Linda said without preamble.

Marsha was quiet for a moment. "How do you feel about that?"

Linda considered the question. "Clear," she said finally. "And sad."

"I'm sorry," Marsha said. "I wish I could say I'm surprised."

"I don't need surprise," Linda replied. "I need honesty."

They talked for a while longer, circling the same themes they had been living inside for weeks now. When they hung up, Linda sat alone in the dark, the quiet pressing in.

She thought of the pastor. She wondered if he would ever know how many conversations had happened around him, how many decisions had been shaped by his endurance rather than his consent.

She also thought of herself. Of the years she had served faithfully, believing that carefulness was synonymous with goodness. Of how slowly, reluctantly, that belief had begun to fracture.

The next morning, Linda wrote her response.

She kept it brief.

After reflection, I don't believe stepping back would be faithful to what I now understand about this situation. If that means my continued participation is not possible, I accept that.

She read it once, then sent it.

The reply came later that day.

Thank you for your honesty. We will take this under advisement.

Linda closed her laptop and leaned back in her chair. She felt a wave of exhaustion wash over her, deeper than anything she had felt during the months of meetings and deliberations. This was not the fatigue of overwork. It was the weariness that came from standing in truth without guarantee of welcome.

A few days later, she received word that she would be stepping off the committee at the end of the month. The language was gracious. The decision framed as mutual.

Linda read the message without anger.

On her final meeting day, she arrived early one last time. She sat at the table and looked around the room, committing small details to memory—the scuffed baseboard, the faint smell of coffee, the way the light fell across the empty chairs.

The meeting proceeded smoothly. Linda spoke rarely. When adjournment came, the chair thanked her publicly for her service. Others echoed the sentiment. Linda nodded, accepted the words, felt their sincerity and their limits.

As she gathered her things, she felt no triumph. No vindication. Only a quiet grief, and beneath it, something steadier.

Outside, the air was warm. Summer had arrived fully now. Linda stood on the steps for a moment, breathing deeply. She felt lighter and heavier all at once.

She knew she had not changed the outcome of the case. The pastor was still waiting. The system still intact. But something in her had shifted irrevocably.

Process, she now understood, could be faithful. It could also be used to avoid faithfulness.

Walking away from the building, Linda felt the cost of having learned that distinction. She also felt its necessity.

There were things she could no longer carry.

And there were things she could no longer pretend not to see.

As she reached her car, Linda did not feel resolved. She felt awake.

And that, she knew, would shape whatever came next—whether the system was ready for it or not.

STORY 4

The Language of Resilience

The first time someone called her resilient, Anna felt seen.

It was said kindly, almost tenderly, in the fellowship hall after worship. A longtime member had taken her hands in his, looked at her with something like pride, and said, "You've handled all of this with such resilience."

Anna smiled, thanked him, and meant it. At the time, the word felt like recognition. It named something real: the long months of tension, the meetings that went nowhere, the careful sermons that tried to hold a fractured room together without splitting it further. Resilience sounded like faithfulness with a backbone.

She carried the word with her for days afterward, letting it settle where encouragement usually did.

It did not stay there.

Over time, resilient began to appear everywhere. In emails from denominational staff. In notes left on her desk. In the annual review where strengths were highlighted before challenges were delicately sidestepped.

Anna continues to demonstrate remarkable resilience in the face of ongoing difficulty.

She read the sentence twice, then once more. The phrasing was familiar, polished. She could imagine it being used for others. She could also feel, dimly, that something was being asked of her without being said outright.

Resilient meant she had not broken.

Resilient meant she could continue.

The congregation's struggles were not new. A prolonged conflict, never fully named, had settled into the life of the church like a low-grade fever.

People still showed up. Programs continued. The building was maintained. From the outside, things looked functional.

From the inside, everything required translation.

Anna spent much of her time absorbing disappointment and redirecting it into language that could be heard. She learned which concerns needed to be softened, which truths needed to be delayed. She carried the emotional residue of meetings that ended politely and conversations that never quite happened.

She told herself this was leadership. She had been trained for this. She had preached often about endurance, about bearing one another's burdens. She believed what she said.

What she had not anticipated was how little space endurance left for protest.

At a presbytery meeting one afternoon, Anna sat near the back, listening as names were lifted up for recognition. A colleague was thanked for stepping into an interim role. Another was praised for navigating a difficult season with grace.

When Anna's name was mentioned, the speaker smiled. "We want to acknowledge Anna for her resilience," he said. "She's been steady in challenging circumstances, and we're grateful."

There was polite applause. Anna nodded, her face warm. She noticed, not for the first time, that the recognition did not come with a question. No one asked what the circumstances were, or why they persisted.

Resilience, she was learning, was a full stop.

Later that week, she met with her supervisor. It was a routine check-in, the kind designed to offer support without intruding too much. They sat across from each other in a small office, sunlight filtering through the blinds.

"How are you holding up?" her supervisor asked.

Anna paused. The question was familiar, well-intentioned. She felt the familiar pull to reassure.

"I'm okay," she said. "Tired, but okay."

Her supervisor nodded. "I'm always impressed by how resilient you are."

The word landed differently this time.

Anna felt a tightening in her chest, subtle but unmistakable. She wondered what would happen if she said, I don't want to be resilient anymore. She wondered how that would be received.

Instead, she smiled. "Thank you."

As she left the office, Anna felt a quiet dissonance settle in. Resilience, she realized, was beginning to function as a ceiling. It named the maximum amount of strain she was expected to endure without changing the conditions that produced it.

That night, she lay awake replaying the day. The compliments. The nods. The absence of curiosity.

She thought of a phrase she had used with parishioners countless times: You don't have to be strong all the time.

She wondered when she had stopped believing it applied to her.

The next Sunday, Anna preached on a familiar text about perseverance. She spoke thoughtfully, carefully, drawing connections between faith and endurance. As she spoke, she felt the words hollow out slightly, as if she were speaking from memory rather than conviction.

After worship, a woman approached her with tears in her eyes. "Your strength means so much to us," she said. "You keep us grounded."

Anna thanked her, hugged her, and felt something inside her wince.

Grounded, she thought, was another word that carried expectation.

In the quiet of her office later, Anna opened her journal, one she had not written in consistently for months. She stared at the blank page, then began to write without censoring herself.

Resilience is being used to excuse what should be addressed.

The sentence surprised her. She read it again, feeling its weight.

She wrote another.

I am praised for surviving what no one is willing to change.

Anna set the pen down and closed the journal. Her hands trembled slightly. She felt exposed, as if she had admitted something dangerous.

For the first time, she allowed herself to consider the possibility that resilience was not neutral. That it could be a way of honoring suffering without interrupting it.

She sat quietly, listening to the hum of the building around her. Somewhere down the hall, a door closed softly. The church continued its life, steady and composed.

Anna took a deep breath. She did not yet know what to do with this insight. She only knew that something had shifted.

Being resilient no longer felt like praise.

It felt like a role she had been cast in without consent.

And she was beginning, slowly, to wonder what it would mean to refuse it.

The word followed Anna into places she hadn't expected.

It appeared in a handwritten note slipped into her mailbox. Thank you for your resilience during this difficult season. It surfaced in a denominational newsletter, her name listed under a brief paragraph about steady leadership. It showed up again in a casual hallway conversation, spoken lightly, almost affectionately.

"You're so resilient," a colleague said, shaking her head with admiration. "I don't know how you do it."

Anna smiled, the expression arriving automatically. Inside, something tightened.

She began to notice how the word functioned socially. It ended conversations before they could deepen. It reassured the speaker that no further response was required. Resilience, once named, absolved others from asking what was being endured or why.

She tested this insight quietly, the way she tested sermons before preaching them. In a meeting with a small group of leaders, she mentioned feeling morally strained rather than tired.

One of them nodded sympathetically. "Well, you've always been strong."

The word strong landed like a translation error.

"I'm not sure strength is the issue," Anna said carefully.

The conversation moved on.

Later that day, she sat alone in her office and replayed the exchange. No one had been dismissive. No one had been unkind. And yet she felt strangely erased, as if the language available to describe her experience had already been chosen for her—and it did not include dissent.

She pulled her annual review from a folder and read it again, this time with a different eye.

Demonstrates resilience in navigating congregational complexity.

Maintains composure under pressure.

Offers steady presence during prolonged uncertainty.

Anna felt a wave of sadness she had not anticipated. None of it was untrue. And none of it acknowledged the cost.

She thought of a meeting from the previous year, one that had left her shaking with anger she never expressed. She thought of the Sunday she had driven home in silence, gripping the steering wheel, unsure whether she could preach another careful sermon without something in her breaking.

Those moments had not been moments of resilience. They had been moments of containment.

That night, Anna dreamed she was standing in a room where everyone was applauding. The sound was loud and unrelenting. She smiled, bowed her head, accepted the praise. When she tried to speak, no sound came out. The applause grew louder.

She woke with her heart racing.

The next morning, she met with a member of the congregation who wanted to talk about the future of the church. He spoke earnestly about vision, about stability, about how grateful everyone was that Anna had "stayed steady" through the past few years.

"We really need you right now," he said. "Your resilience is such a gift."

Anna nodded. She had heard the sentence so many times it no longer sounded like a compliment. It sounded like a contract.

"What would happen," she asked slowly, "if I wasn't resilient?"

He laughed, assuming she was joking. "Well, let's hope we never find out."

She smiled in return, then changed the subject.

As the weeks passed, Anna began to experiment—not outwardly at first, but internally. She stopped translating every discomfort into gratitude. She allowed herself to notice resentment when it arose, rather than spiritualizing it away. She paid attention to the way her body reacted in meetings, the tightness in her jaw, the shallow breath.

Resilience, she realized, had required a kind of dissociation. It asked her to remain functional without remaining fully present to herself.

One afternoon, she met with a younger pastor who had reached out for support. They sat together in Anna's office, sunlight pooling on the rug between them. The pastor spoke haltingly about conflict, about exhaustion, about feeling trapped between expectations and conscience.

"I guess I just need to be more resilient," the pastor said finally, eyes downcast.

Anna felt something shift.

"Who told you that?" she asked gently.

The pastor shrugged. "Everyone."

Anna leaned forward. "What if resilience isn't what's being asked of you?" she said. "What if what you're feeling is a signal, not a failure?"

The pastor looked up, startled. "I've never thought of it that way."

Neither had Anna, not until now.

After the pastor left, Anna sat quietly, letting the conversation echo. She realized that she had been passing along the same language that was constraining her, even as she sought to care for others. Resilience had become the default diagnosis, the catch-all virtue.

That evening, she returned to her journal.

Resilience is praised because it keeps things from changing.

She paused, then added another line.

It is admired because it costs others nothing.

The words felt stark, almost harsh. She did not soften them.

At the next presbytery gathering, Anna sat with colleagues she trusted. When the familiar praise surfaced again—We're so grateful for your resilience—she did something small but deliberate.

She nodded, then said, "I'm grateful for support. Resilience has limits."

The comment landed awkwardly. Someone cleared their throat. Another smiled uncertainly.

"That makes sense," someone said finally. "Well, you know we're here for you."

Anna smiled, but she felt the gap widen between what was offered and what was needed.

Walking to her car afterward, she felt a mix of fear and relief. Naming limits felt risky. It disrupted the script. But it also felt honest in a way she had been missing.

Resilience, she was learning, was not a personal virtue she could simply accept or reject. It was a cultural expectation embedded in the system she served. Refusing it would require more than rest. It would require language, boundaries, and the willingness to disappoint.

She sat in the car for a moment before starting the engine, hands resting on the wheel. She thought of the dream, the applause, the silence.

"I don't want to be applauded anymore," she said aloud. "I want to be heard."

The words surprised her with their clarity.

As she drove away, Anna knew she was stepping into uncertain territory. The praise might thin. The support might prove conditional. She did not yet know how far she was willing to go.

But she knew this: continuing to accept resilience as praise would mean continuing to disappear inside it.

And she was no longer willing to make that trade.

Anna did not announce her refusal. She learned quickly that refusals did not need announcements to be felt.

It began with small shifts. In meetings, when someone praised her steadiness, she did not rush to absorb the compliment. She let it sit. When asked how she was holding up, she resisted the instinct to reassure and answered more precisely.

"I'm carrying a lot," she said once. "And some of it shouldn't be carried alone."

The response unsettled the room in a way she had not intended, but also not regretted. Someone nodded. Someone else changed the subject. The meeting moved on.

Afterward, a colleague pulled her aside. "You okay?" he asked quietly. "You seemed. . . different."

Anna smiled. "I am."

She meant it, though the truth was more complex. Being different meant being slightly out of step, no longer moving in perfect rhythm with expectations she had not consciously agreed to but had nonetheless fulfilled for years.

The next time the word surfaced—in an email from a denominational office thanking her for her resilience during a challenging season—Anna did not reply right away. She stared at the screen, her fingers hovering over the keyboard.

Finally, she typed a short response.

Thank you for your note. I'm grateful for the support I've received. I'm also learning that resilience isn't sustainable without shared responsibility.

She read it twice, then sent it.

There was no reply.

In supervision the following month, the conversation circled familiar ground. Her supervisor asked about workload, about rest, about self-care. Anna answered honestly, then said something she had not planned to say.

"I don't think the primary issue is capacity," she said. "I think it's moral strain."

Her supervisor frowned slightly. "Can you say more about that?"

Anna considered the question. She could hear the temptation to translate, to soften. She resisted.

"I'm being asked to absorb conflict and ambiguity in ways that protect the system but slowly erode my integrity," she said. "Resilience has become the name we give to that erosion."

The room grew quiet.

"That's a serious claim," her supervisor said carefully.

"It is," Anna replied. "And I don't say it lightly."

Her supervisor nodded, thoughtful. "I wonder if you might be personalizing systemic issues."

Anna smiled faintly. "I've been doing the opposite for years."

The meeting ended cordially. Anna left feeling neither validated nor dismissed, but keenly aware of how narrow the space was for this kind of language.

That awareness followed her into the pulpit.

The lectionary text that Sunday was about endurance. Anna had preached it before, had drawn the usual connections between faith and perseverance, suffering and hope. As she prepared the sermon, she found herself unable to take the familiar route.

She wrote and rewrote, crossing out phrases that now felt evasive. She kept returning to a single question: endurance for what, and for whom?

On Sunday morning, the sanctuary was full enough to feel encouraging. Anna stood at the pulpit and took a breath.

"Endurance," she began, "is often praised as a virtue. And sometimes it is. But endurance without truth can become a way of disappearing."

The room was very still.

She spoke carefully, naming the difference between bearing hardship that leads toward life and bearing hardship that preserves patterns that wound. She did not name the congregation's conflict. She did not need to. The words carried their own resonance.

After the service, reactions were mixed. Several people thanked her for the sermon, their voices earnest. One said quietly, "That gave me a lot to think about." Another avoided her gaze entirely.

Later that afternoon, an elder emailed her.

Your sermon today felt unsettling. I'm not sure it was what people needed right now.

Anna read the message, then closed her laptop. She sat for a long moment, feeling the familiar pull to apologize, to explain. She let the moment pass.

That evening, she met with a small group from the congregation, a circle she had trusted for years. They spoke about the sermon, about the tension in the room. One person finally said what others seemed to be circling.

"It sounded like you were saying you can't keep doing this," she said gently.

Anna did not rush to reassure. "I was saying I can't keep doing it the same way," she replied.

There was a pause.

"What would change look like?" someone asked.

Anna shook her head slowly. "I don't know yet. But I know pretending everything is fine isn't it."

The group sat with that, the weight of it settling in.

Walking home later, Anna felt exposed and oddly grounded. The praise had thinned. The room had grown less predictable. And yet, she felt more present than she had in years.

Resilience had asked her to endure quietly. Refusing it required her to speak aloud what endurance had cost.

At home, she opened her journal again.

Resilience kept me acceptable, she wrote.

Truth may make me inconvenient.

She underlined the second sentence.

Anna did not yet know where this path would lead. She did not know whether the system could adjust, or whether she would eventually need to step away. What she knew was this: she could no longer allow her silence to be mistaken for strength.

Resilience had been a language that protected others from discomfort.

Now she was learning a different language—one that did not promise safety, but did promise integrity.

And whatever came next, she would not be praised for it.

She would be changed by it.

The meeting invitation arrived with no agenda.

Anna noticed that immediately. Meetings without agendas were rare, and when they happened, they usually meant someone wanted to talk about something without naming it first. She read the email twice, then accepted.

The meeting was set for midweek, late afternoon. When Anna arrived, the room was already occupied by the executive pastor and the clerk of session. Both smiled warmly, the way people do when they are trying to signal care before delivering uncertainty.

"Thank you for coming," the executive pastor said. "We just wanted to check in."

Anna sat, placing her notebook on the table but not opening it. She had learned when preparation was useful and when it only gave the illusion of control.

"We've been hearing some feedback," the clerk began gently. "About your sermon a few weeks ago. And some of the language you've been using lately."

Anna nodded. "I assumed there would be."

The executive pastor leaned forward slightly. "Some people felt unsettled. Concerned."

"About what?" Anna asked.

There was a pause. Not long, but deliberate.

"About tone," he said. "About whether the congregation is being asked to carry too much."

Anna felt a familiar heat rise in her chest. She kept her voice steady. "I've been carrying that concern for a long time."

"Yes," the clerk said quickly. "And that's part of why we admire your resilience."

There it was again.

Anna exhaled slowly. "I want to be clear," she said. "When resilience is named without addressing what makes it necessary, it becomes a way of avoiding responsibility."

The executive pastor shifted in his chair. "I don't think anyone is trying to avoid responsibility."

"I don't think that either," Anna replied. "But intention doesn't cancel impact."

The room grew quiet. Anna could feel the tension stretching, the careful equilibrium threatened by language that refused to smooth itself.

"What would you want us to do differently?" the clerk asked.

The question was sincere. That made it harder.

Anna considered her answer. She could offer suggestions: mediation, clearer boundaries, shared leadership. All of those were true. None of them were the heart of it.

"I want us to stop praising endurance as if it were the goal," she said. "And start asking what keeps creating the conditions that require it."

The executive pastor nodded slowly. "That's a larger conversation."

"Yes," Anna said. "It always is."

They ended the meeting without conclusions, only acknowledgments. As Anna left the room, she felt the familiar mix of relief and unease. She had spoken clearly. She had not been dismissed. And nothing had changed.

That evening, Anna walked through the sanctuary alone. The lights were low, the space quiet. She sat in the front pew and rested her hands on the worn wood.

She thought about the word resilience again, how it had once felt like encouragement and now felt like a narrowing. She thought about how often faith communities confused endurance with holiness, suffering with calling.

She remembered something an old mentor had once said, years ago, after a particularly difficult season: Just because you can survive something doesn't mean you're meant to.

At the time, Anna had nodded politely and moved on. Now the sentence returned with force.

The following Sunday, a woman approached her after worship. She was not someone Anna knew well, but her expression was intent.

"I wanted to say thank you," the woman said quietly. "For your honesty lately."

Anna waited.

"I've been telling myself for years that I just need to be stronger," the woman continued. "More resilient. But listening to you, I realized I might be confusing faith with endurance."

Anna felt a tightening behind her eyes. "You're not alone in that."

The woman nodded. "I hope you keep saying what you're saying. Even if it makes people uncomfortable."

Anna smiled, the gratitude in her chest mingled with something heavier. "Thank you," she said. "That means more than you know."

Later that afternoon, Anna sat at her desk and reread emails she had archived without much thought over the years. Notes of praise. Commendations. Performance evaluations. The pattern was unmistakable now.

Resilience had been her currency.

It had purchased approval, trust, latitude. It had also kept deeper questions at bay. As long as she remained resilient, no one had to ask whether the system itself was faithful.

She opened her journal again.

Resilience is rewarded because it keeps the peace, she wrote.

But peace without justice is just quiet.

She paused, then added another line.

I am not here to keep things quiet.

The realization settled in her body like a decision she had already made but not yet spoken aloud.

Over the next weeks, the language around her shifted subtly. The praise did not disappear, but it softened, became more cautious. Some people stopped using the word resilience altogether. Others doubled down, invoking it almost defensively.

Anna noticed who leaned in and who pulled back.

She also noticed her own limits more clearly. There were days when the weight of it all pressed down hard, when she longed for the simplicity of being admired rather than questioned. On those days, she reminded herself why she had begun speaking differently in the first place.

Resilience had allowed her to survive.

Truth was allowing her to remain herself.

One evening, as she locked the church doors after a late meeting, Anna paused on the steps and looked back at the building. She loved this place. That had never been in question. What was in question was whether love required her silence.

She did not yet know how this would end. Whether the system would adjust, or whether she would eventually be asked to move on. She only knew that returning to the old language would cost her something she was no longer willing to give.

Resilience had been a role she played well.

She was done performing it.

As Anna walked to her car, the night air cool against her skin, she felt the weight she carried settle differently. Heavier, perhaps. But truer.

And for the first time in a long while, she trusted that distinction to matter.

The shift did not announce itself as conflict. It arrived as distance.

Anna noticed it first in the small things. A meeting she was no longer invited to. A decision shared after the fact rather than discerned together. A conversation that stopped when she entered the room and resumed, awkwardly, after she left.

No one confronted her. No one accused her of anything. The system was too polite for that.

Instead, she felt herself being reclassified.

Where she had once been described as steady, she was now intense. Where she had been resilient, she was now going through something. The language softened, but its effect sharpened. Her concerns were gently bracketed as temporary, emotional, situational.

She recognized the move immediately. She had used it herself, years ago, with others.

Anna found herself grieving not just the change in tone, but the clarity it brought. The admiration she had once received had always been conditional. It had depended on her ability to absorb strain without making it visible. Now that she had refused that role, the admiration had nowhere to land.

One afternoon, she received a request for a meeting with the presbytery liaison. The email was warm, supportive, non-specific. Just wanted to check in.

They met at a neutral location, a coffee shop halfway between offices. The liaison arrived with a practiced smile and an air of concern.

"I've been hearing some things," she said, after they ordered.

Anna nodded. "I assumed you might."

"People are worried about you," the liaison continued. "About whether you're okay."

Anna smiled faintly. "I am."

The liaison tilted her head. "You don't sound very convinced."

"I'm convinced," Anna said. "I'm just not performing wellness the way people expect."

There was a pause.

"I wonder," the liaison said carefully, "whether you might be experiencing some burnout."

Anna felt a familiar temptation to agree, to accept the diagnosis that would make everything simpler. Burnout was legible. Burnout could be addressed with rest, with coaching, with a plan.

"This isn't burnout," Anna said quietly.

The liaison frowned. "How can you be sure?"

"Because rest made this clearer, not easier," Anna replied. "And because what I'm naming isn't exhaustion. It's conscience."

The liaison took a sip of her coffee, buying time. "Sometimes those things overlap."

"Sometimes," Anna agreed. "But this isn't overlap. This is misrecognition."

They sat in silence for a moment, the hum of the café filling the space.

"Well," the liaison said finally, "we want to support you. Perhaps we could explore some additional resources."

Anna nodded. "I'm open to support. I'm not open to having this reduced to self-care."

The liaison smiled thinly. "Of course."

They parted politely. Anna walked to her car feeling neither angry nor relieved. She felt seen just enough to be managed, not enough to be understood.

That night, she dreamed again of applause. This time, when she opened her mouth to speak, the clapping stopped. The room fell silent. People looked at her expectantly.

She woke with her heart pounding.

The next morning, she received an email from the executive pastor asking if she would consider taking a brief leave. Just to give yourself space, it said. No pressure.

Anna read the message several times.

She knew the offer was sincere. She also knew what it functioned as: a way to relocate the problem inside her rather than around her. Leave would provide relief, but it would not address the conditions that made resilience necessary.

She replied simply.

Thank you for the offer. I don't believe time away will resolve what I'm naming.

The response was slower this time. When it came, it was brief.

Understood. Let's keep talking.

Anna closed her laptop and sat quietly. She felt the ground beneath her shifting, the old assurances no longer holding. The path she was on felt narrower, less predictable. And yet, she felt more aligned than she had in years.

That Sunday, she preached again.

This time, she did not speak about endurance. She spoke about truth-telling as an act of care. About how love that refuses to name harm is not gentleness, but avoidance. About how communities are shaped not only by what they celebrate, but by what they are willing to hear.

The room was quiet.

After worship, fewer people lingered. Some avoided her. Others sought her out with gratitude that felt more tentative than before.

One man approached her hesitantly. "I don't know if I agree with everything you're saying," he admitted. "But I think it's important."

Anna smiled. "I can live with that."

Later that afternoon, alone in her office, Anna sat with the weight of it all. She felt grief, yes. Loss of ease. Loss of certainty. Loss of being uncomplicatedly liked.

But she also felt something steadier underneath: a sense that she had stopped trading herself for approval.

Resilience had once been the bridge that allowed her to remain in place. Now it felt like a cul-de-sac, one she had finally turned away from.

She opened her journal one last time that day.

I am not failing because I refuse to endure quietly, she wrote.

I am changing because I refuse to disappear.

Anna closed the journal and stood. Outside, the afternoon light slanted across the sanctuary floor, illuminating dust motes that drifted without urgency.

She did not know what would come next. Whether the system would stretch or whether she would eventually need to leave. What she knew was that whatever happened, it would happen with her eyes open.

Resilience had been praised because it made things easier for others.

She was choosing something else now.

Not ease.

Not admiration.

But integrity.

And for the first time, she trusted that choice to hold—whatever it cost.

The question came, eventually, the way these questions always do—framed as concern, delivered softly, leaving little room to refuse without appearing unreasonable.

The executive pastor asked Anna to meet again. This time, the chair of session was present as well. The room was familiar, the tone measured. Tea had been set out, untouched.

"We want to talk about next steps," the executive pastor began. "For everyone's well-being."

Anna nodded. She had learned how to listen for what was being said and what was being managed.

"There's a sense," the chair continued, "that this season has been especially heavy for you."

"It has," Anna said.

"And that perhaps," the executive pastor added, "the congregation would benefit from a season of stability. From reassurance."

Anna heard the translation clearly now. Stability meant predictability. Reassurance meant quiet.

"What are you asking?" she said.

There was a pause. Not hesitation—coordination.

"We're wondering," the chair said, "whether you might consider reframing some of your language. Less focus on strain. More emphasis on hope."

Anna felt a familiar ache rise behind her sternum. Not anger. Sadness.

"Hope without honesty isn't hope," she said. "It's denial."

The executive pastor sighed. "We're concerned that some of what you're saying is being experienced as destabilizing."

"Yes," Anna replied. "That's often what truth feels like before it settles."

The room grew still.

"No one doubts your commitment," the chair said. "But part of leadership is knowing when to protect the community."

Anna leaned forward slightly. "And part of leadership is knowing when protection becomes avoidance."

The conversation ended as these conversations often do—without resolution, but with lines drawn more clearly than before. Anna left the building feeling the weight of the moment press into her chest.

That evening, she walked through her neighborhood, the air cool and clear. She thought about the years she had given to this place. The baptisms. The funerals. The quiet pastoral moments no one ever saw.

She also thought about the way resilience had once shielded her. How easily she had worn it. How costly it had been.

The next Sunday, Anna did something she had not planned to do until the moment arrived.

At the close of the sermon, she paused.

"I want to say something personal," she said. "And I want to say it carefully."

The room was quiet, attentive.

"For a long time, I've been praised for my resilience. And I've accepted that praise. But I've learned that resilience can sometimes be a way of asking someone to carry what should be shared."

She let the sentence land.

"I'm not naming this to create fear," she continued. "I'm naming it because I believe faithfulness requires honesty—especially when honesty is uncomfortable."

There was no applause. Only stillness.

After worship, reactions were muted but sincere. Some thanked her. Others said nothing. A few looked at her with something like relief.

On Monday morning, Anna wrote a letter.

It was not a resignation. Not yet. It was a letter of discernment, addressed to the session, naming what she could and could not continue to carry. It spoke of shared responsibility, of moral limits, of love that does not require disappearance.

She read it several times before sending it.

The response did not come quickly.

In the days that followed, Anna felt an unfamiliar lightness. The weight had not disappeared, but it had shifted. She was no longer contorting herself to fit the language that kept her acceptable.

When the response finally came, it was careful, grateful, non-committal.

We appreciate your honesty and will take time to discern together.

Anna smiled when she read it. She knew what it meant. Time would be asked for again. Perhaps indefinitely.

But something was different now.

She was no longer waiting for permission to be whole.

Weeks later, sitting alone in the sanctuary one evening, Anna thought about the word resilience one last time. She did not reject it outright. She simply refused to let it be the measure of her faithfulness.

Resilience could be a gift. But only when freely offered, never when demanded.

Anna stood and turned off the lights. As she locked the door behind her, she felt a quiet resolve settle into place.

Whatever came next—staying, leaving, reshaping—she would no longer allow praise to substitute for care, or endurance to replace truth.

She had borne enough.

Now she would insist on being accompanied.

And in that insistence, she sensed, faint but real, the possibility of a different kind of faithfulness—one not built on how much could be endured, but on how honestly life could be lived.

She walked into the night, no longer resilient in the way she once had been.

But more fully present than ever before.

STORY 5

The Good Exit

THE LANGUAGE WAS ALREADY waiting for him.

Before Mark had finished telling the session, before the room had fully absorbed the words I will be concluding my ministry among you, the phrases began to surface—soft, practiced, familiar.

Discerned.

Mutual.

Grateful.

A healthy transition.

Mark watched them arrive as if from a distance, each one placed gently on the table like an offering. Heads nodded. Eyes softened. Someone reached for a box of tissues, though no one was crying yet.

He had known this would happen. He had even rehearsed his part in it.

"I want to say," he began, keeping his voice even, "that this decision comes after a long season of prayer and discernment."

That sentence was true. It was also incomplete.

The chair leaned forward. "We want you to know how grateful we are for your leadership," she said. "And for the way you've handled this process."

Handled, Mark thought, was doing a lot of work.

He nodded. Gratitude was easier to offer than explanation. Gratitude was safe.

The conversation unfolded as expected. Timeline. Communication plan. Farewell events. Someone asked whether he had something lined up next. Mark answered honestly that he did not, which prompted sympathetic murmurs but no alarm. This, too, fit the script. Faith. Trust. Next chapter.

No one asked why staying had become impossible.

When the meeting ended, people lingered, embracing him, thanking him again. "This feels really healthy," someone said, squeezing his arm. "I'm glad we're doing this well."

Mark smiled. He had learned how to do that without effort.

Driving home later, he replayed the meeting in his mind. He noticed how little of it had surprised him. The relief in the room had been palpable, though no one would have named it that way. A good exit allowed everyone to exhale. It offered closure without excavation.

At home, Mark set his bag down and sat at the kitchen table, staring at the wood grain beneath his hands. The house was quiet. His partner would be home later. He welcomed the solitude.

He thought back to the early years in the congregation, when leaving had seemed unthinkable. There had been energy then. Shared vision. The sense that difficult conversations would eventually be had, that tensions would be addressed rather than absorbed.

Somewhere along the way, that confidence had thinned.

Mark could trace the shift through a series of small accommodations. Sermons softened to avoid controversy. Meetings that ended with vague assurances. Conflicts deferred in the name of unity. Each choice made sense on its own. Together, they formed a narrowing corridor.

He had not been pushed out. That was the story everyone would tell, and it would be accurate. He had stayed longer than many would have. He had been praised for his steadiness, his patience, his pastoral heart.

What no one named was the cost of staying faithful inside shrinking moral space.

The next Sunday, Mark stood in the pulpit and preached as he always had—carefully, thoughtfully, attentive to the room. He did not announce his departure yet. There would be time for that. He spoke instead about seasons, about listening for God's movement without forcing it.

After worship, people gathered as usual. Conversations flowed easily. Someone commented on how calm everything felt lately. Another said, "It's good to see us in a better place."

Mark nodded, aware of the irony.

Later that afternoon, an elder stopped by his office. "I just want to say," she said, "I really admire the way you're leaving. No drama. No hard feelings. It says a lot about you."

Mark thanked her. He meant it.

When she left, he closed the door and sat down heavily. The phrase no hard feelings echoed in his mind. He wondered what people imagined feelings were supposed to look like in situations like this. He wondered how anger could ever be expressed when gratitude was the only acceptable currency.

That night, he pulled out a folder he had not opened in months. Inside were notes he had written to himself over the years—fragments of sermons he never preached, questions he never raised, moments he had marked as important and then set aside.

One page caught his attention.

Leaving doesn't mean it didn't matter, he had written.

It means it mattered enough to stop pretending.

He read the lines several times, feeling their truth settle into him.

Over the next weeks, the story of his departure took shape. The announcement was drafted and approved. It spoke of discernment, gratitude, mutual blessing. Mark recognized his own words in it, edited and smoothed.

Emails arrived from colleagues and denominational staff, praising the clarity of the process, the health of the transition. "This is how it should be done," one wrote.

Mark wondered how many people had left quietly and been told the same thing.

At the farewell reception, the room was full. There were speeches and laughter, stories from the early days. Someone joked about how hard it would be to replace him. Another spoke of legacy.

When Mark stood to respond, he thanked them sincerely. He named what he loved about the congregation. He spoke of hope for what would come next.

He did not speak of what had made leaving necessary.

As the evening wound down, people hugged him goodbye, promising to stay in touch. Mark smiled, held their hands, felt the warmth of their care. It was real. And it was incomplete.

Driving home later, the weight of the evening settled over him. He felt both lighter and heavier than he had expected. Lighter for having made the decision. Heavier for everything that would remain unsaid.

A good exit, he realized, was a kind of mercy. It allowed everyone to move forward without rupture. It preserved dignity. It protected relationships.

It also left important truths untouched.

Mark parked the car and sat for a moment before going inside. He thought about what it would mean to bless this ending honestly—to hold gratitude and grief together without resolving the tension between them.

He did not know yet how to do that.

What he knew was this: leaving faithfully did not erase the harm that had accumulated, and being blessed did not mean being healed.

As he turned off the engine, Mark took a deep breath. The night was quiet, the air cool. Tomorrow, the work of leaving would continue, orderly and kind.

And somewhere beneath that kindness, the weight he carried would remain—unacknowledged, but real.

This, too, he thought, was part of the cost of a good exit.

The announcement was read aloud the following Sunday.

Mark sat in the front pew as the clerk of session stood at the lectern, holding the printed statement with both hands. The language sounded slightly different when spoken aloud—rounder, more complete, as if the words themselves believed what they were saying.

After a season of prayerful discernment. . .

With gratitude for shared ministry. . .

A mutual decision. . .

Mark listened carefully, noticing which phrases landed with ease and which ones skimmed the surface. Around him, people nodded. A few sighed audibly. Someone behind him whispered, "That makes sense."

When the clerk finished, there was a moment of quiet, then a gentle ripple of applause. Not loud. Respectful. Appropriate.

Mark stood when it was his turn to speak. He looked out over the congregation he had served for nearly a decade. Faces he knew well looked back at him—some tearful, some relieved, most composed.

"I want to echo what's been said," he began. "This congregation has meant a great deal to me. I'm deeply grateful for the ministry we've shared."

The words came easily. Gratitude was not the hard part.

"As we enter this transition," he continued, "I hope we can do so with trust—trust in God's leading and in one another."

He paused, feeling the weight of everything he was not saying.

"Thank you," he concluded. "For your care, and for your faithfulness."

He sat down to another round of polite applause.

After worship, the narthex filled quickly. People approached him with hugs, handshakes, words of affirmation.

"I'm really impressed by how you're handling this," one man said.

"This feels very healthy," another added.

"You're setting such a good example," a third offered.

Mark smiled, thanked them, felt the phrases slide over him like a well-worn garment.

One woman, a longtime member, held his hands tightly. "I know this must be hard," she said. "But it's good to see you leaving on such good terms."

Mark nodded. "It is hard," he said.

She smiled, seemingly reassured, and moved on.

Later that afternoon, Mark sat with his partner on the back porch, the late summer air warm and still.

"How are you really?" she asked.

Mark considered the question. He had been asked it many times already. This was the first time it felt safe to answer honestly.

"I feel. . . clean," he said slowly. "Like I've done everything right."

"And?" she prompted gently.

"And I feel like the story everyone's telling about this isn't the whole story," he added.

She nodded. "Does that matter?"

Mark stared out at the yard, the grass needing to be cut, the edges of the garden just beginning to blur.

"I think it does," he said. "Because if this is remembered as healthy, then nothing needs to be learned from it."

The next few weeks unfolded in a blur of activity. Transition plans. Final meetings. Farewell lunches. Each interaction reinforced the same narrative: gratitude, closure, blessing.

Mark noticed how often people thanked him for making this easy.

He wondered when leaving had become something that needed to be easy for those who stayed.

In a final meeting with the session, the chair spoke warmly about legacy and continuity. "You've given us such a gift," she said. "By handling this so graciously."

Mark nodded. "I wanted to be faithful."

"And you have been," she replied quickly. "In every way."

The certainty in her voice closed the door on further conversation.

After the meeting, Mark returned to his office and began packing books into boxes. He moved slowly, touching spines, remembering conversations sparked by certain titles. He found a notebook tucked behind a shelf, one he had forgotten about.

Inside were reflections from a particularly difficult year. Questions he had asked himself late at night. Anger he had never expressed aloud. Pages where the handwriting grew sharp, almost jagged.

He sat on the floor and read until the light shifted.

None of this, he realized, would make it into the story of his departure.

And yet, it was as much a part of his ministry here as anything that would be named.

At the farewell reception, the speeches were warm and generous. People laughed at familiar stories. Someone presented him with a framed photograph of the church building at sunset.

When Mark stood to respond, he felt the familiar pull to resolve everything cleanly.

"I'm grateful," he said again, and meant it. "For the relationships, the trust, the shared work."

He paused, just long enough for something else to surface.

"I hope," he added, carefully, "that as you move forward, you'll continue to listen—not just for what's comfortable, but for what's true."

The room was quiet for a moment. Then someone clapped, and the moment passed.

Driving home later that night, Mark felt the accumulated weight of the weeks press in. He had done everything asked of him. He had not made things harder. He had not demanded explanations or named harms that would complicate the narrative.

He had given the congregation a good exit.

What he was less certain about was whether he had given himself one.

At home, he sat alone in the dark living room, the boxes stacked neatly along the wall. He thought about how quickly his absence would be normalized, how soon the vacancy would become a process rather than a person.

He did not regret leaving. That certainty surprised him with its steadiness.

What he grieved was the way leaving had been framed as resolution rather than reckoning.

A good exit, he was beginning to understand, was not the same as a truthful one.

It allowed everyone to move on.

It did not require anyone to look back.

Mark turned off the light and went upstairs, carrying with him the quiet knowledge that while his departure had been blessed, something essential had been left behind—unnamed, unhealed, and still waiting to be acknowledged.

This, too, he knew, was part of the story.

Even if it would never be told aloud.

The weeks between the announcement and Mark's final Sunday stretched oddly, both crowded and hollow.

Every day brought another reminder that he was already becoming past tense. People spoke to him with a slightly altered tone, as if he were both present and gone. Decisions were made without him—not abruptly, but gently, the way one stops setting a place at the table before the absence is fully felt.

Mark understood the logic of it. Transition required momentum. Lingering sentiment could slow things down.

Still, the quiet acceleration unsettled him.

He noticed it most in meetings. Where his voice had once carried weight, it now landed lightly, politely acknowledged and then set aside. Not dismissed—just no longer central. He found himself listening more than speaking, observing the system rehearse life without him.

In one final staff meeting, a colleague spoke enthusiastically about "the freedom this transition opens up." Another nodded, adding, "There's a sense of relief, honestly. Not about you—but about clarity."

Mark smiled, because that was what was expected.

Relief, he thought, was an honest word. It was just never spoken in his presence before.

Later that afternoon, a younger staff member knocked on his office door. She hovered awkwardly, then stepped inside.

"I hope this isn't weird," she said. "But can I ask you something?"

"Of course," Mark replied.

"Do you think leaving like this—so well—is actually better?" she asked. "Or does it just make it easier for everyone else?"

The question caught him off guard with its precision.

"I think," Mark said slowly, "that it does both. And those two things aren't the same."

She nodded, absorbing that. "I keep wondering what would happen if people didn't leave so cleanly."

Mark smiled faintly. "Then the system would have to ask harder questions."

She thanked him and left. Mark sat back, feeling the truth of the exchange settle into him. It was the closest thing to honesty he had experienced all week.

That night, Mark dreamed he was packing boxes that refilled themselves as soon as he taped them shut. Books returned to shelves. Papers slid back into drawers. No matter how methodically he worked, nothing stayed packed.

He woke frustrated, the dream clinging to him longer than usual.

The next day brought another round of farewells. Lunch with a group of elders. Coffee with a longtime member. Each conversation followed a familiar arc: appreciation, reminiscence, reassurance.

At one lunch, someone said, "You're doing this the right way."

Mark looked up. "What would the wrong way be?"

There was a brief, uncomfortable laugh. "Oh, you know. Anger. Blame. Hard feelings."

Mark nodded. "Those are certainly harder."

No one responded.

Driving home afterward, Mark realized how narrow the acceptable emotional range had become. Gratitude was permitted. Sadness, if tidy, was allowed. Anger was suspect. Moral protest was out of bounds.

A good exit required emotional discipline.

As his final Sunday approached, Mark worked carefully on his farewell sermon. He wanted it to be true without being incendiary, generous without being evasive. He revised sentence after sentence, trimming anything that sounded like indictment.

In the end, the sermon focused on calling and trust—on releasing one another without denial. He preached it calmly, his voice steady, the sanctuary quiet.

At the benediction, he felt the weight of it press through him, a mix of relief and grief that did not resolve.

After worship, someone approached him with tears in their eyes. "You've made this so easy for us," she said. "Thank you for that."

Mark held her hands. "I'm glad I could."

He wondered, not for the first time, who us included.

The farewell reception that afternoon was warm, efficient, full of good intentions. Cards. Gifts. A cake with his name carefully spelled. People hugged him and spoke of prayers and gratitude.

One person said, "You'll always be part of our story."

Mark smiled. He wondered what part.

When it was time to leave, he walked through the building one last time. His office was empty now, the walls bare. The sanctuary lights were off. The space felt smaller without people in it, less charged.

He paused at the door and rested his hand on the frame. He felt no bitterness, no urge to turn back.

What he felt was a quiet ache for what had never been named.

At home that evening, Mark and his partner sat together on the couch, the house unusually quiet.

"You did it," she said. "You made it through."

"Yes," Mark replied. "I did."

"Do you feel done?" she asked.

He considered the question carefully. "I feel finished," he said. "I don't feel resolved."

She nodded, understanding.

That night, Mark wrote one last entry in his notebook.

A good exit keeps the peace, he wrote.

It does not tell the whole truth.

He closed the notebook and set it aside.

Mark did not regret choosing dignity. He did not wish he had scorched the earth or spoken every grievance aloud. He knew that would not have been faithful to who he was.

But he also knew that the goodness of the exit had come at a cost.

The system would remember his departure as exemplary. It would not have to ask why exemplary departures were necessary.

Mark lay in bed, the house quiet around him, and allowed himself to feel the full complexity of what he was carrying. Gratitude and grief. Relief and loss. Integrity and unfinished truth.

Leaving well, he realized, did not mean leaving whole.

It meant leaving with what you could carry.

And trusting yourself enough to name what you could not.

The first Monday after Mark's final Sunday arrived with a clarity he had not expected.

He woke at his usual time out of habit, then lay still, listening to the quiet of the house. There was no sermon to refine, no meeting agenda waiting in his bag. The absence felt clean, almost startling. For a moment, he let himself enjoy it.

By midmorning, the quiet had changed shape.

Mark drove into town anyway, parking farther from the church than he ever had before. He walked the familiar streets without a destination, noticing how quickly the building receded into the background of ordinary life. People passed him, unaware that something had ended.

At a coffee shop, he ran into a former elder. They exchanged warm greetings, then the elder smiled and said, "I hear everything went really well yesterday."

"Yes," Mark replied. "It did."

"That's such a gift," the elder continued. "Not everyone gets to leave that way."

Mark nodded. "I know."

They talked for a few more minutes, about weather and travel plans. As they parted, the elder added, "You should feel proud."

Mark smiled politely, then watched him go.

Pride, he thought, was not what he felt.

Back home, Mark opened his laptop and scanned emails out of reflex. His inbox was quieter than it had been in years. A few notes had arrived overnight—thank-yous, blessings, reminders that prayers continued.

One message stood out. It was from a denominational leader he respected.

I just want to commend you on such a faithful transition. You modeled what healthy leadership looks like.

Mark stared at the screen for a long moment. He did not doubt the sincerity of the message. He also felt its weight settle uneasily in his chest.

Healthy leadership, he thought, had become synonymous with not disturbing anyone on the way out.

He closed the laptop.

That afternoon, Mark sorted through boxes in the garage. He found old bulletins, youth retreat folders, handwritten notes from parishioners dating back years. Each one carried a memory, a moment of genuine connection. He felt gratitude rise easily, unexpectedly.

He also felt the ache of knowing that gratitude did not cancel what had made leaving necessary.

As he worked, his partner came home early and joined him, sitting on the concrete floor among the boxes.

"You're quiet," she said.

"I'm thinking," Mark replied.

"About what?"

"About how quickly this became a success story," he said. "And how little space there is in that story for what actually happened."

She nodded. "People like clean endings."

"Yes," Mark said. "Especially when they don't have to examine their part in why someone left."

Later that evening, Mark received a call from a colleague who was still serving in the denomination. They talked easily at first, catching up on family and travel plans. Eventually, the colleague said, "I've been meaning to ask—how did you know it was time?"

Mark considered the question. He could offer the polished answer. Discernment. Prayer. Trusting God's leading.

Instead, he said, "I knew when staying started to require me to pretend I didn't know what I knew."

There was a pause on the line.

"That sounds hard," the colleague said finally.

"It was," Mark replied. "And leaving didn't make it disappear. It just made it honest."

After they hung up, Mark sat quietly, the room dim around him. He realized how rare it was to speak that plainly, and how much energy it took to keep such language contained.

The next Sunday, he attended worship at a different church. He sat in the back, anonymous, letting the liturgy wash over him without responsibility. When the pastor preached about calling and sacrifice, Mark listened with a new attentiveness.

He wondered how many people in the room were enduring things they did not have language for. How many were being praised for resilience, patience, flexibility—virtues that asked them to absorb what should be addressed.

After the service, someone greeted him warmly and asked if he was new. Mark smiled and said yes.

Walking back to his car, he felt a small release. Not belonging, he realized, could be a kind of rest.

That afternoon, Mark opened his notebook again. He had avoided it since the farewell. Now he turned to a blank page and began to write.

A good exit protects the institution, he wrote.

It does not necessarily protect the truth.

He paused, then added another line.

If departure is always framed as health, then injury never has to be named.

The words felt sharp but steady.

Mark knew he would not be invited to correct the story being told about his leaving. He would not be asked to complicate it, to add nuance or cost. The narrative was already in circulation, doing its work.

And perhaps, he thought, that was inevitable.

But it did not mean he had to internalize it.

As evening settled in, Mark sat on the porch, watching the light fade. He felt no urge to rush toward what came next. For the first time in years, the future did not feel like a problem to solve.

Leaving well, he was learning, had preserved relationships and protected dignity. It had also left him carrying a truth that had nowhere to land.

He could live with that.

What he could not live with was pretending that a good exit was the same as a healed one.

As darkness fell, Mark breathed deeply, letting the weight of that distinction settle into him. He did not know where his path would lead next. He only knew that wherever he went, he would carry the lesson with him.

Some endings are clean.

Some are faithful.

Rarely are they the same.

And learning to tell the difference, Mark suspected, would shape the rest of his life.

The narrative settled faster than Mark expected.

Within a month, the vacancy was being discussed in procedural terms. A search committee was forming. A profile would be written. Dates were named. The congregation moved forward with admirable efficiency.

Mark heard about it indirectly—through friends, through denominational updates, through the quiet shorthand of people who assumed he was ready to be past it. Each piece of information landed with a small thud, not painful exactly, but disorienting.

He realized how quickly a person becomes a process once they leave.

One afternoon, he ran into the former clerk of session at the grocery store. They greeted each other warmly, exchanged pleasantries about weather and travel. As they were about to part, she said, "Things are going really well, actually. People are feeling hopeful."

Mark smiled. "I'm glad to hear that."

She hesitated, then added, "I think the way you left really helped."

Helped, Mark thought. The word hovered between gratitude and relief.

"That's good," he said.

Driving home, he felt a familiar tightening in his chest. Not resentment—something closer to sadness. The goodness of the transition had become proof that the departure itself required no further reflection.

He began to see how the story functioned.

If the exit was healthy, then the system was healthy.

If the transition was smooth, then the past must not have been too damaging.

If the pastor left well, then whatever pain existed had been resolved by leaving.

The logic was clean. And it erased him.

One evening, Mark met with a former parishioner who had asked to talk before he "got too settled into what's next." They sat at a quiet restaurant, the kind where conversations felt protected by ambient noise.

"I wanted to ask you something," she said after they ordered. "But I didn't know if it was appropriate."

Mark smiled. "You can ask."

"Did we fail you?" she asked quietly.

The question caught him off guard—not because it was accusatory, but because it was honest.

Mark took a breath. "I don't think failure is the right word," he said slowly. "But I do think there were things we couldn't face together."

She nodded, eyes downcast. "It didn't feel like we were allowed to talk about that."

"No," Mark agreed. "It didn't."

They sat in silence for a moment.

"I keep wondering," she said, "if calling it a good ending means we don't have to learn anything."

Mark met her gaze. "That's what worries me too."

When they parted, Mark felt both lighter and heavier. Lighter for having spoken plainly. Heavier for knowing how rare such conversations were.

In the weeks that followed, Mark noticed how often people assumed he was at peace. Friends asked how retirement—or whatever came next—was treating him. Colleagues spoke of his exit as exemplary, something to aspire to.

He realized that the story now belonged to others.

His own experience—ambivalent, unfinished, morally complex—had no official place to live.

One afternoon, he sat with his partner on a park bench, watching people walk dogs and push strollers.

"Do you ever want to correct them?" she asked. "When people talk about how healthy it all was?"

Mark considered the question. "Sometimes," he said. "But I don't think that's my work anymore."

"What is?" she asked.

Mark watched a child wobble uncertainly on a bicycle, a parent jogging close behind without touching.

"To tell the truth where it's safe," he said. "And to stop carrying what isn't mine."

That night, Mark returned to his notebook. He reread entries from the months before he left—the confusion, the anger, the careful self-correction. He noticed how often he had written about not wanting to hurt anyone.

I didn't want to be the problem, one line read.

He turned the page and wrote something new.

I wasn't the problem. But leaving allowed the problem to remain unnamed.

The words felt neither bitter nor righteous. They felt accurate.

As the season turned, Mark began to imagine what it might mean to tell these stories differently—not publicly, not as critique, but as testimony. To speak honestly about leaving without turning it into either failure or success.

He thought of younger pastors watching exits like his, absorbing the lesson quietly: If you must leave, do it cleanly. Do it gratefully. Don't make trouble on the way out.

He wondered what it would mean to give them a different inheritance.

One afternoon, he received an email from someone he barely knew, a pastor in another region.

I heard about your transition, the message read. I'm in a similar place. I don't know how to leave without feeling like I've failed.

Mark read the email twice. He felt a familiar ache, but also a sense of purpose sharpen.

He wrote back carefully.

Leaving doesn't always mean failure, he typed. Sometimes it means you've reached the edge of what faithfulness can look like in a particular place.

He paused, then added:

And leaving well doesn't mean leaving without wounds.

He sent the message and sat back, feeling something settle into place.

The good exit had done its work. It had preserved dignity, prevented rupture, allowed others to move on.

Now Mark was doing different work.

He was learning to live with an ending that was faithful but unfinished—to resist the pressure to resolve what had not been resolved, to honor the truth without demanding an audience for it.

A good exit, he now understood, was not the end of the story.

It was simply where one version of the story stopped being told.

And what came next—quiet, uncelebrated, morally serious—might matter just as much.

Mark stopped thinking of the departure as something that had happened and began to experience it as something that continued.

It showed up in ordinary moments. In the hesitation before introducing himself to new people. In the way he scanned rooms for familiar dynamics even when none were present. In the reflex to soften his language, to make endings sound cleaner than they were.

Leaving, he was learning, did not conclude the moral story. It relocated it.

Several months after his final Sunday, Mark attended a denominational gathering as a guest rather than a leader. He sat near the back, his name no longer printed on a badge that carried authority. People greeted him warmly, some with curiosity, others with admiration.

"You handled that transition beautifully," one colleague said, clapping him lightly on the shoulder. "It's become something of a model."

Mark smiled. "I've heard that."

"Well," the colleague continued, "it gives people hope. Shows that things don't have to end badly."

Mark nodded, letting the comment pass. He had learned when to resist and when to receive without correction. Still, the word model lingered uncomfortably.

During a break, Mark found a quiet corner and sat with a cup of coffee, listening to conversations drift past him. He heard snippets about vacancies, about pastors "not making it," about churches that were "just too difficult."

He noticed how rarely anyone spoke about moral cost. How easily departures were sorted into success or failure, health or dysfunction. The space between those categories remained largely uninhabited.

A younger pastor approached hesitantly. "Can I ask you something?" she said.

"Of course," Mark replied.

"I'm trying to figure out whether leaving would mean I gave up too soon," she said. "Everyone keeps pointing to your situation as an example of doing it right."

Mark studied her face, the strain just visible beneath her composure.

"Doing it right," he said slowly, "doesn't always mean doing it without pain."

She frowned slightly. "Then what does it mean?"

"It means telling the truth to yourself," Mark said. "Even if the story others tell is simpler."

She nodded, absorbing that. "Thank you," she said quietly, then moved on.

Mark sat back, feeling the weight of the exchange. He realized that his good exit had become a kind of silence others were being asked to emulate.

That evening, back home, he took out the notebook again. He had been returning to it more often now, not out of urgency, but out of attentiveness. He flipped through earlier entries, tracing the arc from confusion to clarity to departure.

On a blank page, he wrote:

A good exit keeps the peace by containing the truth.

Faithfulness asks what truth still needs care afterward.

The words felt steady, unforced.

In the weeks that followed, Mark began to speak differently when asked about his time in the congregation. He did not lead with gratitude alone, though gratitude remained. He also named limits. Strain. The way certain questions had never found room.

He did not offer this language everywhere. He learned to discern where honesty could be received and where it would be dismissed as unnecessary complication. He no longer felt compelled to correct every version of the story.

What mattered was that he no longer corrected himself.

One afternoon, walking through a park near his home, Mark passed a church with its doors open. Music drifted out—rehearsal for a service, perhaps. He paused, listening, then continued on. He felt no pull to enter, no ache of belonging.

Instead, he felt a quiet recognition: his life was no longer organized around making institutions feel good about themselves.

That realization brought both freedom and grief.

Later that night, Mark and his partner sat together, sharing a simple meal.

"Do you think you'd ever say it publicly?" she asked. "What it really cost?"

Mark considered the question. "Maybe," he said. "But not as an accusation. As testimony."

She nodded. "That feels right."

The season turned again. Leaves fell. New pastors were installed elsewhere. Mark's name surfaced less often in denominational conversation. He found work that felt honest, if quieter. He learned what it meant to carry moral seriousness without a role to validate it.

One evening, an email arrived from the same pastor he had written to months earlier.

I left, the message read. Not cleanly. Not quietly. But honestly. It's been hard—and it feels right.

Mark sat with the message for a long time before replying.

I'm glad you listened to yourself, he wrote back. Leaving doesn't finish the work. It just makes room for a different kind of faithfulness.

He sent the message and closed his laptop.

The good exit, Mark now understood, had been necessary. It had protected relationships, preserved dignity, and allowed him to step away without destruction.

It had not healed what had been injured. It had not taught the system what it refused to learn.

And that was not a failure.

It was simply the truth.

As he prepared for bed that night, Mark felt no urge to resolve the tension he carried. He had stopped mistaking resolution for wholeness. What he carried now was something else: a settled willingness to live without tidy endings.

Some stories, he realized, are meant to be closed gently.

Others are meant to be held open.

And faithfulness, at least for him, meant knowing the difference—and refusing to confuse blessing with repair.

The good exit had been an ending.

What followed was something quieter, less admired, and more demanding.

A life lived with the truth still intact.

And for Mark, that was enough.

STORY 6

After the Blessing

THE BLESSING HAD BEEN generous, public, and final.

Hands laid gently on shoulders. Words chosen with care. Gratitude spoken slowly, as if pacing itself might make the ending easier to bear. When it was finished, there had been applause—soft, respectful—and then movement. People stood. Chairs scraped. The room reorganized itself around what came next.

Daniel stood still a moment longer than necessary.

He did not want to rush the leaving. He had learned, too late perhaps, that endings completed too efficiently had a way of erasing things that still mattered.

Outside, the air was cool and clear. It was early evening, the kind of light that made everything look briefly resolved. Daniel breathed deeply, feeling the unfamiliar looseness in his body. No agenda. No next obligation. No one watching to see how he would carry himself now.

The first days after leaving felt strangely clean.

He woke without urgency. He drank coffee slowly. He noticed how quiet the house was midmorning, how the day opened without demanding explanation. Friends checked in, congratulated him on "doing it well," assured him that rest would come now.

Rest did come.

What did not come was relief.

Daniel noticed it first in small ways. A tightening in his chest when someone asked what he was doing now. A hesitation before answering a simple question about the past. He realized he was still translating—softening language, choosing words that would reassure rather than reveal.

"I had a good ministry," he would say.

"It was time for a transition."

"I'm grateful for how it ended."

All of that was true. None of it explained why the weight had followed him.

One afternoon, he found himself standing in the grocery store aisle staring at a shelf without seeing it. His mind had drifted back to a meeting from years earlier—one that had ended politely, with decisions deferred. He remembered how he had nodded, how he had gone home and slept badly, how he had told himself this was simply leadership.

The memory passed, but the feeling lingered.

Daniel paid for his groceries and sat in his car longer than necessary before driving home. He rested his forehead briefly against the steering wheel.

"This was supposed to be over," he said aloud.

But what, exactly, was this?

The institution had closed the chapter. The farewell had been spoken. The blessing had done its work. No one expected him to still be carrying anything from that season.

And yet, without the daily demands of ministry, the questions he had postponed now surfaced with clarity.

Why had certain conversations never happened?

Why had silence been rewarded as maturity?

Why had endurance been praised when it required him to shrink?

These were not questions he could bring back to anyone now. The system had moved on. The relationships had been preserved, in part, because nothing too sharp had been named.

Daniel began to understand something unsettling: leaving had protected others from having to reckon with what he was now reckoning with alone.

At night, he slept lightly. Not badly—just alertly. He woke with fragments of memory rather than anxiety. A hallway conversation. A sermon he had edited mid-delivery. A moment when he had chosen not to speak because the room could not receive it.

He did not regret those choices. That surprised him.

What surprised him more was how little space there was to talk about them now.

When people asked how he was doing, they expected gratitude. When he mentioned feeling unsettled, they offered reassurance.

"Of course it feels strange," someone said. "You gave so much of yourself."

Another added, "It takes time to decompress."

Daniel nodded. He did not disagree. He simply sensed that something else was happening—something deeper than fatigue.

One morning, he pulled out a box of old journals he had not opened in years. He sat on the floor and began reading entries from the middle years of his ministry. The handwriting shifted from careful to cramped. The tone moved from hopeful to precise, then to guarded.

One entry stopped him.

I don't know how to say this without making it worse.

He stared at the sentence for a long time.

That, he realized, had been the problem all along. Not that he lacked insight. Not that he lacked courage. But that the truth he carried could not be spoken without consequence—and he had been tasked, implicitly, with minimizing those consequences for others.

Daniel closed the journal and leaned back against the wall. He felt neither anger nor bitterness. He felt something quieter and harder to hold: grief for the self who had learned to manage moral weight without witness.

In the weeks that followed, Daniel noticed how often people assumed that leaving had resolved everything.

"You must feel so free now," someone said.

"Are you enjoying the rest?" another asked.

"Yes, and yes," Daniel replied. He meant it.

What he did not say was that freedom without context felt thin, and rest without recognition felt incomplete.

One afternoon, he met with a therapist at the suggestion of a friend. The first session passed gently, the usual questions asked and answered. Near the end, the therapist said, "What do you think you're grieving?"

Daniel opened his mouth, then closed it again.

"I don't think I'm grieving the job," he said slowly. "I think I'm grieving the years I spent carrying things I was never meant to carry alone."

The therapist nodded. "That sounds like moral injury."

The phrase landed with unexpected precision.

Daniel did not respond right away. He felt something inside him settle—not relief, exactly, but recognition. A naming that did not demand repair or redemption.

"Yes," he said finally. "That's it."

Walking home afterward, Daniel felt a quiet shift. Nothing had been fixed. Nothing had been reframed into success. But something had been acknowledged without being smoothed over.

After the blessing, he was learning, there was still work to be done.

Not the work of returning.

Not the work of explaining.

But the work of integrating a life that had been lived faithfully inside constraints that had exacted a cost.

That work would not be visible. It would not be celebrated. It would not be mistaken for resilience.

It would be slow. Honest. And mostly solitary.

As Daniel unlocked his door and stepped inside, he felt the weight he carried settle—not lighter, but clearer. For the first time since leaving, he did not feel behind himself, rushing to catch up to a story already told.

He was finally standing where he was.

After the blessing.

And still living with what remained.

The weeks took on a different texture once Daniel stopped expecting them to feel better.

He still woke without an alarm. He still noticed the luxury of unclaimed hours. But the initial sense of suspension—of being briefly unmoored between identities—gave way to something heavier and more specific. He was no longer disoriented. He was attentive.

Without the daily demands of ministry, Daniel began to notice how often his inner life had been organized around anticipation. Preparing for meetings. Anticipating reactions. Anticipating the need to soften, clarify, reassure. Anticipation had been a form of vigilance, and vigilance had passed for faithfulness.

Now, there was nothing to anticipate.

And in that absence, what surfaced was not peace, but residue.

He noticed it when he tried to read. His eyes moved across the page, but his mind drifted to conversations he had never finished. When he went for walks, he caught himself rehearsing explanations no one had asked for.

When he met new people and they asked what he did, he felt a brief, irrational pulse of panic—followed by relief when the answer no longer mattered.

"I was a pastor," he would say.

Past tense felt strange in his mouth. Not painful. Just unfinished.

One afternoon, Daniel agreed to meet a former colleague for lunch. They had not worked closely, but had known each other long enough to speak easily. The colleague congratulated him again on "how well everything ended" and asked what was next.

"I don't know yet," Daniel said.

"That must feel freeing," the colleague replied.

Daniel hesitated. "It feels. . . quiet."

The colleague smiled, misunderstanding him kindly. "You've earned the rest."

Daniel let it pass.

Walking home afterward, he realized how difficult it was to describe what he was experiencing without sounding ungrateful or unstable. There was no language in common circulation for the afterlife of moral seriousness. People understood exhaustion. They understood grief. They understood relief.

They did not understand the unsettled clarity that came when the noise stopped.

That evening, Daniel returned to the journals again. He read entries from the later years, noticing how carefully he had written, how much he had already known.

One entry stood out.

I am not confused. I am constrained.

He remembered writing it late at night, feeling both brave and frightened. He had closed the journal afterward and not opened it again for months.

Now, reading it again, he felt a surge of compassion for the person he had been. He had not lacked insight. He had lacked room.

Daniel began to see that what lingered after leaving was not trauma in the dramatic sense. It was something quieter: the accumulation of moments where he had chosen containment over expression, prudence over truth, because that was what love had seemed to require at the time.

The institution had praised him for that discernment.

No one had asked what it cost.

In therapy, the sessions deepened slowly. The therapist did not rush him toward meaning or solutions. She listened as Daniel named memories he had never spoken aloud—not because they were forbidden, but because they had never felt actionable.

"There's no villain in these stories," Daniel said once, frustrated. "Just a lot of people trying not to make things worse."

The therapist nodded. "That's often where moral injury lives," she said. "Not in betrayal, but in chronic compromise."

The phrase settled into Daniel with weight and relief.

He began to notice how often he had internalized responsibility for outcomes he could not control. How frequently he had absorbed institutional anxiety as personal failure. Leaving had ended the role, but it had not ended the reflex.

One morning, Daniel caught himself apologizing to no one in particular for feeling angry.

He laughed out loud when he realized what he was doing.

"Who am I apologizing to?" he asked the empty room.

There was no answer. And that, oddly, helped.

As the months passed, Daniel's days found a gentler rhythm. He took on part-time work that did not require moral translation. He reconnected with friends outside ministry, people who did not need him to be careful with his words.

Still, the moral questions persisted—not intrusively, but insistently.

What would it have meant to speak sooner?

What would have broken if he had refused silence earlier?

What had he protected—and at whose expense?

He learned not to push these questions away. He also learned not to force answers.

One afternoon, sitting in a park, Daniel watched a group of people setting up folding chairs for an event. They moved efficiently, practiced hands unfolding metal frames, aligning rows. The scene stirred something in him—a familiar mixture of appreciation and unease.

He realized then that what he missed was not leadership, or even belonging.

It was being witnessed in the act of carrying weight.

In ministry, there had been at least the illusion of shared burden, even when the reality fell short. Now, the carrying was solitary. Necessary. Honest.

That evening, Daniel wrote in a new notebook—one not burdened with the voice of his former self.

After the blessing, he wrote, there is no one left to reassure.

He paused, then continued.

That doesn't mean there is nothing left to tend.

The insight felt important. The work now was not to explain or justify what had happened, but to integrate it into a life that no longer needed to perform coherence for others.

He began to think of moral injury less as something to be healed and more as something to be held with care—like a scar that altered movement without defining it entirely.

Late one night, Daniel received an email from a former parishioner. It was brief, thoughtful.

I hope you're doing well. I just wanted to say thank you—for things I didn't understand at the time.

Daniel read it twice. He felt a quiet warmth, followed by a familiar restraint. He resisted the urge to reply with reassurance or explanation.

Instead, he wrote back simply.

Thank you for saying that. I hope you're well too.

He closed his laptop and sat quietly.

The institution had blessed his leaving. The community had moved on. The story had been told cleanly and put away.

What remained was this slower, truer work—learning how to live without having to make sense of everything for anyone else.

Daniel did not yet know where it would lead.

But for the first time, he trusted that the work itself was faithful—even without witnesses, even without resolution.

After the blessing, the silence was not empty.

It was full of unfinished life.

And he was finally allowing himself to listen to it.

Daniel discovered that time behaved differently now.

Without deadlines to anchor it, days expanded and contracted unpredictably. Some passed quickly, filled with ordinary tasks and quiet satisfaction. Others stretched thin, each hour carrying more weight than seemed reasonable.

He learned not to judge either kind.

One morning, he volunteered at a community food pantry—a practical decision, modest, untheological. He wanted to do something useful without needing to interpret it for anyone. The work was simple: sorting donations, stocking shelves, greeting people briefly and kindly.

For the first hour, he felt fine. Grounded. Present.

Then a woman thanked him with an intensity that startled him. "You're very kind," she said, holding his gaze longer than necessary.

Daniel felt the old reflex surge—to reassure, to downplay, to make the moment lighter. He caught himself mid-motion.

"You're welcome," he said simply.

As she walked away, he felt the familiar ache return—not because of the interaction itself, but because he recognized how long he had trained himself to manage others' emotional responses. Even now, without the role, the training remained.

That afternoon, he felt unexpectedly tired.

Not physically. Morally.

He sat at home and tried to name the feeling. It wasn't sadness, exactly. It wasn't anger. It was the fatigue of no longer having a framework that explained why things were hard.

In ministry, difficulty had always come with narrative scaffolding. Seasons. Call. Sacrifice. Discernment. Even pain could be metabolized into purpose.

Now there was no such structure.

Daniel began to understand that part of what he was grieving was the loss of meaning-making authority. He no longer had access to a shared language that told him what his suffering was for.

At first, that felt like loss.

Later, it began to feel like honesty.

In therapy, he spoke about the temptation to rush toward interpretation. "I keep wanting to explain what this is," he said. "To make it productive."

The therapist nodded. "What if it doesn't need to be productive?"

The question landed quietly but firmly.

Daniel sat with it for several days.

He noticed how often institutions required pain to justify itself—through growth, through insight, through visible outcome. He had absorbed that requirement deeply. Pain without explanation had always felt irresponsible.

But now, explanation itself felt suspect.

One evening, Daniel attended a small gathering of former clergy—people who had left for different reasons, at different times. The conversation was cautious at first, polite, filled with updates about work and family.

Then someone said, "I didn't realize how angry I was until after I left."

Heads nodded.

Another added, "I thought leaving would fix it. Instead, it clarified it."

Daniel felt a quiet recognition bloom in his chest. He spoke less than usual, listening carefully. For the first time since leaving, he did not feel unusual for carrying unresolved weight.

No one rushed the conversation toward hope. No one offered tidy conclusions. They spoke of regret and relief, loyalty and loss, without forcing coherence.

Driving home afterward, Daniel realized how rare that kind of space was.

Not healing space. Honest space.

He slept deeply that night.

The next morning, he woke with a sense of something loosening—not resolving, but settling. He felt less pressure to make the past legible. Less urgency to determine what it all meant.

He returned to his notebook.

I don't need to redeem what happened, he wrote.

I need to stop arguing with it.

The sentence surprised him. It felt like permission.

Over the next weeks, Daniel practiced a different posture. When memories surfaced, he let them come without evaluation. When emotions arrived without explanation, he resisted the urge to assign them meaning.

Some days, this felt peaceful. Other days, it felt empty.

Both were acceptable.

He noticed subtle changes. His speech slowed. His laughter came more easily. He stopped apologizing reflexively. He began to trust that silence did not always require filling.

One afternoon, walking through his neighborhood, Daniel passed a church just as the bells began to ring. He stopped and listened, the sound familiar and distant at once.

For years, the bells had marked his time. Now they simply rang.

He felt no longing to return. No resentment. Just a quiet awareness of having lived a life that had required more endurance than anyone had known.

And now, a life that required something else.

Integration, he was learning, was not about stitching the past into a coherent story. It was about allowing contradiction to remain without forcing it into resolution.

He did not need the ending to make sense.

He needed it to be true.

That evening, Daniel sat on his porch as dusk settled in. He watched the light fade, the world growing indistinct at the edges. He felt no urgency to move inside.

After the blessing, there were no markers to tell him when the work was done.

But he was beginning to understand that the work itself—quiet, uncelebrated, unfinished—was not a failure of faithfulness.

It was its continuation.

And for now, that was enough to keep living.

Daniel began to understand that the hardest part was not remembering.

It was not knowing where the memories belonged.

In ministry, memory had always had a place. Stories were shared in supervision, processed in prayer, woven into sermons or quietly set aside as pastoral wisdom. Even the difficult moments found containment within a role that could absorb them.

Now, memory arrived without a container.

One morning, while washing dishes, Daniel was suddenly back in a committee room from years earlier. He could see the table clearly, the legal pads, the careful posture of the chair. He remembered the exact moment when he had chosen not to speak—not because he lacked conviction, but because he could already see the outcome.

The memory passed. The dish slipped slightly in his hand and clinked against the sink.

Daniel turned off the water and sat down heavily at the kitchen table.

He realized that what lingered was not regret. It was something closer to unwitnessed fidelity—choices made for the sake of care that had never been named as such, and now had no place to be acknowledged.

Later that day, he met with a friend who had never been part of church life. They had known each other since college, before Daniel had entered ministry. Over coffee, the friend asked casually, "Do you miss it?"

Daniel paused longer than usual.

"I miss being understood without explanation," he said finally.

His friend frowned slightly. "I don't think I know what you mean."

"That's okay," Daniel replied, smiling faintly. "I'm not sure I did either."

The friend nodded, accepting the answer without pressing. Daniel felt grateful for that restraint. He was learning that not every truth needed translation—and that some truths lost their shape when forced into clarity too quickly.

In the following weeks, Daniel noticed a subtle but persistent urge to re-enter—not into ministry, but into moral usefulness. He found himself scanning job postings that carried responsibility without authority, care without entanglement. Teaching roles. Consulting work. Anything that allowed him to remain morally serious without being morally absorbed.

He was cautious with himself.

He knew how easily purpose could become anesthesia.

One afternoon, during a therapy session, he named this tension aloud.

"I don't want to disappear," he said. "But I also don't want to recreate the same conditions in a different form."

The therapist nodded. "That's discernment," she said. "Not avoidance."

The distinction mattered more than he had expected.

Daniel began to see how often people confused staying engaged with staying faithful. For years, he had accepted that confusion as inevitable. Now he was learning to live without it.

Still, there were days when the absence of structure felt unkind.

On one such day, Daniel attended a memorial service for someone he had known tangentially through denominational work. The liturgy was familiar, the words practiced. He sat near the back, letting the service unfold without participation.

As the final hymn ended, he felt a swell of emotion—not grief for the person, but grief for the role he no longer inhabited. He missed the steadiness of ritual, the clarity of knowing what was expected of him in moments like this.

Outside, after the service, he stood alone while others gathered in clusters. No one sought him out for pastoral presence. No one looked to him to interpret the moment.

For the first time, he was simply another person standing with loss.

The realization was both freeing and disorienting.

That evening, Daniel wrote again.

After the blessing, he wrote, I am no longer needed in the same way.

He paused, then added:

This is not a failure. But it is a loss.

The words felt right.

As months passed, Daniel noticed that the moral weight he carried was no longer acute. It had become something like a constant pressure—present, shaping, but no longer overwhelming.

He learned how to make room for it.

Some days, that meant long walks without purpose. Other days, it meant conversations that did not aim for resolution. He began to trust that living faithfully did not require him to arrive anywhere in particular.

One evening, he received an invitation to preach at a small congregation that knew his story only vaguely. He considered it carefully.

The invitation stirred both longing and caution.

In the end, he declined—not out of fear, but out of honesty. He was not ready to re-enter a space that would require him to translate his experience into something palatable.

He wrote back kindly, without explanation.

After sending the email, he felt a quiet sense of integrity settle into place.

Later that night, Daniel sat on his porch again, watching the neighborhood settle into darkness. He listened to distant sounds—cars passing, a dog barking, someone laughing nearby.

Life continued, unburdened by his story.

And somehow, that was acceptable now.

He no longer needed the institution to carry what he carried. He no longer needed blessing to legitimize his experience.

What he needed was time—time to let moral seriousness reshape his life without demanding justification.

After the blessing, there was no return to normal.

There was only this slower, truer inhabiting of a self who had chosen care over ease, truth over performance.

Daniel breathed deeply, the night air cool in his lungs.

He did not know what the next season would bring.

But he knew this: the work he was doing now—quiet, invisible, unremarkable—was not a detour from faithfulness.

It was faithfulness itself, continuing on without applause, without audience, without the comfort of being told it was enough.

And for the first time since leaving, that knowledge did not feel heavy.

It felt real.

Daniel realized, gradually, that moral injury did not fade. It thinned.

It stopped demanding his attention in sharp, intrusive ways and began to live closer to the surface of ordinary life. It shaped how he made decisions. How quickly he trusted. How carefully he noticed power and silence in rooms he entered.

It became a way of seeing.

One afternoon, Daniel was invited to serve on the board of a local nonprofit. The work was aligned with his values, the commitment modest. The invitation felt affirming—an acknowledgment that his experience still mattered.

At the first meeting, he sat quietly, listening. The conversation moved quickly, efficiently. A difficult decision arose about funding priorities. People spoke with care, using language of stewardship and sustainability.

Daniel felt the familiar tightening in his chest.

He recognized the moment immediately: the narrowing of options, the careful avoidance of naming who would be harmed by the decision being discussed. He could already see how the conversation would resolve—technically sound, morally costly.

He said nothing.

Driving home afterward, Daniel felt unsettled. Not because he had remained silent, but because he understood why he had. He was no longer constrained by role or consequence. Silence had not been required of him.

And yet, the reflex remained.

That evening, he returned to his notebook and wrote:

Leaving ended the obligation.

It did not erase the training.

The insight felt important.

Daniel began to understand that moral injury was not something that stayed behind in institutions. It traveled with people. It showed up in new spaces, quietly shaping behavior long after the original context was gone.

This realization was sobering—but also clarifying.

He began to practice something small but deliberate. When he noticed the impulse to self-censor without necessity, he paused. He asked himself a simple question:

What would it cost to speak here?

Sometimes the answer was too much. Sometimes it was nothing at all. Learning the difference felt like learning a new language.

At the next board meeting, when a similar decision arose, Daniel spoke.

Not dramatically. Not accusatorily.

"I think we should name who this impacts," he said calmly. "Even if the decision stays the same."

The room grew quiet for a moment. Then someone nodded. Another person added a clarifying question. The conversation shifted—not resolved, but widened.

Afterward, a board member approached him. "Thank you for that," she said. "I hadn't realized what we were skipping over."

Daniel felt a small, steady satisfaction—not triumph, not relief, but alignment.

He realized then that the work after moral injury was not withdrawal or constant vigilance. It was recalibration—learning when silence was discernment and when it was residue.

In therapy, he named this shift.

"I don't want to become someone who avoids responsibility because I've been hurt," he said. "But I also don't want to disappear again."

The therapist nodded. "That's moral maturity," she said. "Not innocence. Not armor. But discernment shaped by experience."

The phrase stayed with him.

Daniel noticed how often people expected him to be either healed or broken. Either ready to return or permanently wounded. There was little room for the reality he inhabited: changed, attentive, carrying knowledge that could not be undone.

One evening, Daniel attended a lecture at a local college. The topic was ethics in public life. The speaker spoke eloquently about values, integrity, courage.

During the question period, someone asked about moral compromise.

The speaker responded confidently. "We all make compromises," he said. "What matters is staying true to our core."

Daniel felt the familiar tension rise. The answer was not wrong—but it was incomplete.

After the lecture, Daniel walked home slowly. He thought about how often moral injury occurred not because people abandoned their values, but because they tried to live them inside systems that made coherence impossible.

He thought about how little language existed for that experience.

At home, he wrote again.

Moral injury is not about losing values, he wrote.

It is about being required to live them in pieces.

The sentence felt like something he might someday share. Or not. He no longer felt pressure to decide.

As the year turned, Daniel felt himself becoming more grounded. Not lighter. More rooted. The questions no longer startled him. They arrived like familiar companions, asking to be acknowledged rather than answered.

He found that he laughed more easily now. That joy returned in ordinary ways—in cooking, in conversation, in moments that asked nothing of him.

And yet, the seriousness remained.

One afternoon, he ran into a former parishioner at the farmer's market. They greeted each other warmly, exchanged updates. As they were about to part, she said, "I hope you know you mattered."

Daniel met her eyes. "Thank you," he said. "I do."

The words surprised him with their truth.

After the blessing, he had learned to live without institutional affirmation. What he was learning now was how to live without disowning what he knew.

Moral injury had not made him cynical. It had made him careful.

Careful with language.

Careful with power.

Careful with himself.

That carefulness no longer felt like a burden.

It felt like a form of integrity that had survived constraint and now lived freely—not loudly, not heroically, but faithfully.

As evening settled, Daniel sat once more on his porch, the world moving quietly around him. He felt no urgency to resolve the past, no need to explain it away.

He was still living after the blessing.

And the life unfolding now—attentive, honest, unfinished—felt like something he could remain in.

Not healed.

But whole enough.

And that, he knew, was not nothing.

The change did not arrive as a revelation. It came as permission.

Daniel noticed it one morning as he stood at the kitchen counter, sunlight cutting across the floor. He had been thinking about nothing in particular—just the ordinary tasks of the day—when it occurred to him that he was no longer bracing himself.

For years, he had lived with a subtle internal posture of readiness. Ready to explain. Ready to absorb disappointment. Ready to carry what others could not or would not. Even after leaving, that posture had remained, shaping his days quietly.

Now, without warning, it loosened.

He did not feel lighter, exactly. He felt unburdened from anticipation. The future no longer presented itself as something he needed to manage preemptively. It could simply arrive.

Daniel sat down at the table and let the moment pass without trying to interpret it.

Later that day, he met a former colleague for coffee. They had not seen each other since Daniel left ministry. The conversation was warm, cautious at first, then more relaxed.

"I've been wondering," the colleague said finally, "do you miss it?"

Daniel considered the question carefully.

"I miss parts of it," he said. "But I don't miss the way I had to disappear in order to stay."

The colleague nodded slowly. "That makes sense."

There was no attempt to reframe his answer, no reassurance offered. Daniel felt unexpectedly grateful.

Walking home afterward, he realized how rare that response had been in his life. How often people rushed to soften truth, to resolve discomfort. He no longer felt compelled to do that work for them.

That evening, Daniel returned to the notebook one last time. He reread the early entries from after his departure—the confusion, the vigilance, the careful naming. He could see now how much of that writing had been an effort to orient himself after losing the institutional frame that once held his life together.

He turned to a blank page.

After the blessing, he wrote, I thought I would be finished.

He paused, then continued.

What I am learning is that I am finished performing.

The sentence felt complete.

Daniel closed the notebook and placed it on the shelf, not as something to be preserved or hidden, but as something that had done its work.

Over the following weeks, he noticed small but meaningful shifts. He stopped explaining himself to strangers. He declined invitations that required him to be a symbol rather than a person. He accepted others without needing them to validate his choices.

When people asked what he did now, he answered simply.

"I'm living," he said.

Sometimes they laughed, assuming humor. Sometimes they nodded, unsure what to say. Daniel no longer felt the need to clarify.

One afternoon, he received an email from someone still in ministry—someone he barely knew.

I heard you left, the message read. I'm starting to realize I may need to as well. Everyone keeps telling me to rest. But rest hasn't fixed what's wrong.

Daniel read the email slowly. He felt the familiar weight rise, then settle.

He wrote back carefully.

Rest helps when you're tired, he typed. But when something feels morally wrong, rest often just makes that clearer. You're not failing if you notice that.

He hesitated, then added:

You don't owe anyone a clean story.

He sent the message and closed his laptop.

The exchange stayed with him. Not as responsibility, but as recognition. He could accompany others now—not by advising, not by fixing, but by refusing to collude with narratives that erased cost.

That, he realized, was the work that remained.

Not leadership. Not repair. But witness.

Witness to what it takes to live faithfully inside constraints. Witness to what lingers after institutions move on. Witness to the truth that blessing does not undo injury, and that injury does not negate faithfulness.

One evening, Daniel attended a small gathering of friends. They sat around a table, eating simply, talking about ordinary things. At one point, someone asked what he was grateful for.

Daniel thought for a moment.

"I'm grateful," he said, "that I no longer have to make my life make sense to everyone else."

The room was quiet for a beat. Then someone nodded. Another smiled.

Later, walking home under a darkening sky, Daniel felt a steady calm settle over him. Not happiness, not resolution—but alignment.

After the blessing, he had learned to live without applause. Without certainty. Without the need to translate moral seriousness into acceptable language.

He had also learned that moral injury did not require him to withdraw from life. It required him to live it differently.

More slowly.

More honestly.

With fewer defenses and clearer limits.

The weight he carried was still there. It always would be. But it no longer defined him, and it no longer demanded that he disappear.

Daniel reached his door and paused, the key in his hand. He thought briefly of the man he had been at the beginning of ministry—earnest, hopeful, unaware of how much he would be asked to absorb.

He did not regret that life.

He simply knew now what it had cost.

And knowing that, he stepped inside—not healed, not restored, but present to himself in a way he had never been before.

After the blessing, the work had continued.

Not in institutions.

Not in roles.

But in the quiet, durable act of living with integrity intact.

That, Daniel understood now, was not an ending.

It was a way forward.

STORY 7

The One Who Stayed

Everyone assumed Miriam would be there.

When committees were formed, her name appeared without discussion. When conflict surfaced, someone always said, "Let's ask Miriam what she thinks." When things threatened to unravel, her presence alone seemed to calm the room.

Miriam had been in the system a long time. Long enough that people forgot when she arrived. Long enough that continuity had become part of her identity. She was not flashy, not loud, not especially visible outside the circles that mattered. She was simply reliable.

And reliability, in this place, was a form of power.

She arrived early for the meeting, as she usually did, placing her folder neatly on the table before taking her seat. The room filled slowly. Greetings were warm, familiar. Someone joked about how long they'd all been doing this together.

Miriam smiled. She always did.

The agenda was predictable. Reports. Updates. A difficult situation near the end, framed carefully under the heading discernment. Miriam scanned the language without surprise. She knew how this would go.

The case had been ongoing for months. A pastor under strain, a congregation divided, a process stretched thin but technically intact. There were no good options. Everyone agreed on that. And agreement, Miriam knew, could be dangerous.

As the conversation unfolded, she listened closely. She noticed who spoke and who did not. She noticed how certain facts were named obliquely, softened before they ever reached the table. She noticed the familiar tightening in her chest as the room circled around what could not be said plainly.

At one point, a colleague turned toward her. "Miriam, what's your sense?"

It was a genuine question. They trusted her.

She could feel the weight of the moment settle in her body. She knew exactly what she thought. She also knew the consequences of saying it.

If she spoke plainly, the room would stiffen. Defensiveness would rise. The conversation would slow, then close ranks. If she spoke carefully—if she translated truth into something survivable—the meeting would move forward. No one would feel exposed. The pastor at the center of the case would continue to carry the strain.

Miriam chose her words.

"I think," she said slowly, "we need to remain mindful of the process and the pressures everyone is under."

Heads nodded. Pens moved. The room exhaled.

The conversation continued.

No one noticed the cost of her restraint. No one ever did.

After the meeting, a colleague lingered as others filed out. "Thanks for that," he said quietly. "You always know how to keep things from escalating."

Miriam smiled again. "I try."

She walked back to her office with the familiar mix of relief and unease settling in. She had done what was expected. She had protected the system. She had kept the conversation from breaking open.

She told herself, as she often did, that staying made a difference.

At her desk, she closed the door and sat still for a moment. The quiet pressed in. She noticed how tired she felt—not exhausted, not overwhelmed, just worn in a particular way. A weariness that came from constant calibration.

She thought about the pastor they had discussed. She thought about the way his options had narrowed over time, how staying faithful had begun to look like absorbing harm quietly. She recognized the pattern because she lived inside it herself.

Miriam had stayed when others left.

She had stayed through leadership changes, policy shifts, public controversies. Each time, she had told herself that her presence mattered—that continuity was a form of care.

And it was. That was the truth that made everything else harder.

She remembered the first time she had considered leaving. Years ago now. A moment when a decision had crossed a line she could not quite name. She had gone home unsettled, restless, unable to sleep.

The next morning, she had returned anyway.

"There are people who need you," she had told herself. "If you leave, who will protect them?"

That logic had carried her forward more times than she could count.

Over time, it had become instinct.

In the afternoon, Miriam met with a younger colleague who was struggling. They spoke candidly, carefully. The colleague asked questions Miriam recognized as dangerous ones—questions that could not be answered honestly without consequence.

Miriam offered guidance that was gentle, prudent, incomplete.

Afterward, she sat alone and felt the familiar ache of dissonance. She was helping. She was also teaching survival.

She wondered, briefly, what she was passing on.

That evening, as she prepared to leave, she noticed the building was quieter than usual. The lights dimmed. The hum of the system slowed. She paused at her office door and looked back once more, taking in the orderly space.

People often thanked her for staying.

They called it loyalty. Faithfulness. Commitment.

Rarely did anyone ask what staying required her to give up.

Miriam locked her door and walked down the hall. Her footsteps echoed softly. She felt the weight she carried settle into its usual place—manageable, familiar, unnamed.

She told herself, as she always did, that she would know when it was time to leave.

What she did not yet know was that staying, too, had a cost—and that cost had been accumulating quietly, beneath the praise, beneath the stability, beneath the assumption that presence was the same as agency.

For now, she stayed.

And in staying, something in her continued to narrow—slowly, carefully, faithfully—without anyone ever calling it harm.

Miriam learned early how to read rooms.

She could tell within minutes which conversations were safe and which ones required translation. She noticed posture, pacing, the slight tightening around people's mouths when a topic drifted too close to something dangerous. Long before others named concern, she felt it in her body.

This skill was praised as wisdom.

It was also how she survived.

Later that week, she sat in her office reviewing notes from a pastoral review process she had helped design years earlier. The process was solid—fair, thorough, defensible. It protected institutions from rash decisions and individuals from arbitrary judgment.

It also took time.

Time, Miriam knew, was not neutral.

The pastor under review had been in limbo for nearly a year. Each extension had been justified. Each delay had been framed as care. The pastor remained technically supported, but practically suspended—unable to move forward, unable to speak freely, unable to leave without consequence.

Miriam traced the arc with painful familiarity.

This is how harm happens without intention, she thought.

During the next committee meeting, the case returned to the table. New information had surfaced. Nothing dramatic. Nothing that changed the outcome. But enough to sharpen what everyone already knew.

As discussion opened, Miriam felt the now-familiar pressure build. She knew where the conversation would land if left untouched. She also knew how easily it could be deflected into procedural language.

Someone said, "We have to be careful here."

Another added, "We don't want to set a precedent."

A third offered, "The process exists for a reason."

Miriam listened. She felt the narrowing again.

She could say it. She could name what was happening—that the pastor was being slowly injured by waiting, that clarity delayed was not neutral, that protection for the system was becoming exposure for the individual.

She could say it.

Instead, she asked a question.

"I wonder," she said, "how we're accounting for the human cost of extended discernment."

The room went quiet—not hostile, but alert.

"That's hard to quantify," someone replied carefully.

Miriam nodded. "Yes," she said. "It is."

The conversation shifted slightly, then returned to safer ground. The decision remained unchanged. Another extension. Another check-in. Another promise to revisit.

Afterward, a colleague pulled her aside. "That was helpful," he said. "You raised the issue without making it accusatory."

Miriam smiled, the familiar ache rising behind her eyes.

Helpful, she thought. And insufficient.

Driving home that evening, Miriam replayed the meeting. She noticed how easily she had calibrated her words, how instinctive the restraint had become. She also noticed the fatigue that followed—not from the meeting itself, but from the constant internal negotiation.

She had once believed that staying meant resisting harm from within.

Now she wondered whether staying had simply made her better at containing it.

At home, she poured a glass of water and stood at the counter without drinking it. She felt the weight of years settle around her—not as regret, but as recognition.

She thought about colleagues who had left. Some abruptly. Some quietly. Some with anger that had startled her at the time.

She had judged them gently, privately.

They couldn't do what needed to be done, she had thought. They didn't see the whole picture.

Now she wondered whether they had seen something she had learned not to.

The next morning, Miriam met with a younger leader she mentored. The conversation turned, as it often did, to discernment and limits.

"I don't know how much longer I can do this," the younger woman said, voice low. "Every option feels wrong."

Miriam recognized the language immediately.

"What feels most wrong?" she asked.

The woman hesitated. "That I'm starting to feel numb," she said. "Like I'm adapting instead of choosing."

The words struck Miriam with unexpected force.

She wanted to reassure her. To normalize the feeling. To frame it as growth.

Instead, she paused.

"That's important to notice," she said carefully. "Numbness can be protective—but it can also be a signal."

"A signal of what?" the woman asked.

Miriam met her eyes. "That the cost is becoming internal."

The woman exhaled, relief and fear mingling in her expression. "What did you do," she asked, "when you started feeling that way?"

Miriam felt the weight of the question settle heavily between them.

She could offer the usual counsel. Patience. Perspective. Trust.

She chose something else.

"I stayed," she said honestly. "And I learned how to carry it."

The woman waited, sensing there was more.

"I don't know yet," Miriam added, "whether that was wisdom or endurance."

The silence that followed was thick but respectful. Miriam realized how rarely she spoke that plainly—even with herself.

After the woman left, Miriam sat alone for a long time. She stared at the notes on her desk, at the systems she had helped build and sustain. She felt pride, and she felt grief.

She had stayed to protect others. That much was true.

She had also stayed to avoid the rupture that leaving would cause—to the institution, to her identity, to the fragile goods that still existed.

She began to see how staying had slowly narrowed what she allowed herself to want.

That evening, walking to her car, Miriam paused under a streetlight. She felt tired in a way that sleep would not touch. Not burned out. Not disillusioned.

Morally compressed.

She wondered how many others lived like this—praised for stability, admired for endurance, quietly losing access to parts of themselves that once spoke clearly.

She had not been silenced.

She had adapted.

And adaptation, she was beginning to understand, could be its own form of injury—especially when it was mistaken for faithfulness.

Miriam drove home slowly, the road familiar beneath her tires. She did not yet know what this recognition would demand of her.

But she knew this much:

Staying had not kept her unchanged.

And the cost of continuity was no longer invisible—even to her.

Miriam began to notice how often people spoke to her in the language of preservation.

"We'd be lost without you."

"You're the steady one."

"You hold things together."

Each phrase was offered as gratitude. Each one carried an unspoken expectation: do not move.

She felt it most acutely when change was discussed—policy revisions, leadership transitions, moments when something genuinely new might be attempted. Eyes turned toward her not for vision, but for reassurance. Her role was not to imagine differently, but to confirm that whatever was proposed would not disturb the fragile equilibrium.

She had become a stabilizing presence.

She had also become a limit.

At a retreat later that month, Miriam sat with a group of senior leaders as they reflected on the state of the system. The facilitator invited them to name both strengths and vulnerabilities. People spoke earnestly about trust, history, resilience.

When it came time to name vulnerabilities, the room grew cautious.

"We're stretched," someone said.

"There's a lot of complexity," another added.

"People are tired," a third offered.

All true. All incomplete.

Miriam felt the familiar pressure rise. She knew what was missing. She also knew how quickly the room would constrict if she named it.

The facilitator turned to her. "Miriam?"

The invitation was gentle. The expectation was not.

She took a breath.

"I think," she said slowly, "we're carrying more moral tension than we're willing to acknowledge. And it's showing up as caution."

The room was quiet.

"Can you say more?" the facilitator asked.

Miriam could feel the edge clearly now. She could step forward—or she could soften.

"I mean," she continued, choosing her words carefully, "that we're very good at managing risk. We're less practiced at naming cost. And sometimes those two things are not the same."

There it was—close enough to truth to be felt, far enough away to remain survivable.

A few people nodded. Someone wrote something down. The conversation moved on.

Later, during a break, a colleague approached her. "That was important," he said. "You always know how to name things without blowing them up."

Miriam smiled, then excused herself.

She walked outside and stood alone, the autumn air sharp and bracing. She realized, with a clarity that surprised her, that she was tired of being trusted for her restraint.

Not because restraint was wrong.

But because it had become the only thing anyone expected from her.

That evening, alone in her hotel room, Miriam lay awake replaying the day. She thought about the younger leaders watching her—learning what was possible, what was permissible, what was rewarded.

She wondered what they were being taught by her staying.

The next morning, she skipped the early session and went for a walk instead. The path wound through trees just beginning to turn. She walked slowly, deliberately, feeling the ground beneath her feet.

She thought about the ways staying had shaped her over time. How she had learned to speak in gradients rather than declarations. How she had trained herself to anticipate resistance and preempt it with caution.

None of this had been demanded explicitly.

It had simply worked.

At some point along the path, Miriam stopped and sat on a bench. She felt something rise that she had not allowed herself to feel in years.

Anger.

Not hot. Not explosive. Just present.

Anger at how much had been asked of her quietly. Anger at how often her staying had been interpreted as agreement. Anger at how rarely anyone had asked what it cost her to keep showing up as the one who could handle it.

She did not push the feeling away.

Instead, she let it sit beside her.

Back at the retreat, the final session focused on hope. People spoke warmly about the future, about resilience and adaptation. Miriam listened, feeling a strange detachment.

She realized that she no longer wanted to be the one who reassured others that everything would be okay.

Not because she believed it wouldn't be.

But because she no longer believed reassurance was the most faithful response.

On the drive home, Miriam felt the weight of the recognition settle in. Staying had allowed her to protect others, to buffer harm, to prevent rupture.

It had also required her to absorb moral tension without release.

She wondered how long she could continue doing that without losing something essential.

That evening, she opened a notebook she rarely used anymore. She did not know what she would write.

After a long pause, she wrote a single line.

Staying has asked me to become smaller than I am.

She stared at the sentence, feeling its truth reverberate.

She was not ready to leave. Not yet. She knew that. There were still people she felt responsible for, still goods she was not willing to abandon.

But something had shifted.

She could no longer pretend that staying was neutral.

She could no longer accept praise for endurance without questioning what endurance was costing her—and others who learned by watching her.

Miriam closed the notebook and sat quietly. The house was still. The world outside continued on, indifferent to her reckoning.

She felt no urgency to act.

But she felt awake.

For the first time, staying did not feel like the obvious choice. It felt like a decision—one that would need to be made again and again, with eyes open.

And that awareness, she sensed, would change everything that followed.

The question arrived without ceremony.

Miriam was halfway through a routine meeting when a colleague—newer to the system, earnest, not yet fully trained in its rhythms—said, "Can I ask something directly?"

The room shifted. Not alarmed. Alert.

"Of course," the chair replied.

The colleague glanced around, then back at Miriam. "I'm trying to understand how we decide when staying becomes harmful," she said. "Not just for individuals, but for the system."

The question landed with more force than anyone seemed to expect.

There was a pause. Papers rustled. Someone cleared their throat.

"Well," the chair said carefully, "that's not always clear."

Miriam felt the familiar internal movement—the instinct to step in, to translate, to rescue the room from discomfort. She could already feel the words forming, the careful phrasing that would lower the temperature.

She did not speak.

The silence stretched.

"I guess what I'm asking," the colleague continued, emboldened now, "is whether we ever ask what staying costs—not just what it preserves."

Miriam felt something tighten, then loosen.

Before she could stop herself, she spoke.

"I think that's the right question," she said.

Heads turned toward her.

"We talk a lot about commitment," Miriam continued, her voice steady but unguarded. "About faithfulness over time. But we rarely ask how much moral compression that requires—or who absorbs it."

The room was very still now.

"This system," she went on, "functions because some people learn to carry unresolved tension quietly. We praise that. We call it stability. But it isn't free."

No one interrupted her.

Miriam felt a strange mix of fear and relief. She had not raised her voice. She had not accused anyone. And yet, she had crossed a line she had respected for years.

The chair spoke slowly. "Are you saying that staying is harmful?"

"I'm saying," Miriam replied, "that staying can be faithful and injurious at the same time. And if we don't name that, we teach people that harm is just part of the calling."

The meeting did not collapse. No one stormed out. The conversation moved on, cautiously, but it did not return to its earlier ease.

Afterward, several colleagues thanked her quietly. One said, "I've been thinking that for a long time." Another said, "That was brave."

Brave was not how it felt.

It felt overdue.

Later that day, Miriam sat alone in her office, the door closed. She felt the familiar post-meeting fatigue, but something else too—a kind of exposure. She had spoken plainly without cushioning the impact. The system had not rejected her for it.

That surprised her.

She wondered how many times she had assumed the room could not bear truth when what it really could not bear was disruption to its habits.

That evening, Miriam received an email from the colleague who had asked the original question.

"Thank you," it read simply. "For answering honestly."

Miriam stared at the message longer than necessary. She felt a quiet ache—gratitude mixed with grief. She wondered what that colleague would learn in the years ahead. What adaptations she would be praised for. What truths she might be taught to hold quietly.

She did not reply immediately.

Over the next few weeks, Miriam noticed subtle shifts. She was still trusted. Still relied upon. But there was a new attentiveness around her, a slight caution. Some people spoke more carefully in her presence. Others avoided certain topics altogether.

She had not become unsafe.

She had become unpredictable.

That, she realized, was often what happened when someone stopped performing their role flawlessly.

One afternoon, she was asked—politely, carefully—whether she might consider stepping back from a particular committee "to make room for emerging leadership."

The request was reasonable. It was also revealing.

Miriam nodded. "I think that's wise," she said.

Walking back to her office, she felt the familiar pull of responsibility tug at her. Part of her wanted to resist, to insist on staying involved to protect outcomes. Another part felt something close to relief.

She was beginning to understand that staying did not have to mean holding everything.

That night, she wrote again.

Staying has taught me how to endure, she wrote.

I am now learning how to choose.

The difference mattered.

Miriam did not decide to leave. Not then. She was not ready, and she was honest about that. There were still relationships she was unwilling to abandon, still places where her presence made a difference she could not ignore.

But staying no longer felt inevitable.

It felt provisional.

She began to imagine what it might mean to stay differently—to refuse certain forms of containment, to name cost more often, to let some things break rather than absorbing the strain herself.

This imagining was quiet, tentative. She did not share it widely.

For the first time, she did not feel obligated to.

One evening, as she locked her office and walked down the familiar hallway, Miriam paused beneath the dim lights. She felt the accumulated weight of years press against her—not as a burden she needed to escape, but as something she could finally acknowledge.

Staying had shaped her.

It had also taken something from her.

Both were true.

And now, at last, she was allowing herself to hold that truth without smoothing it over, without translating it into reassurance, without pretending that continuity alone was a moral good.

She stepped outside into the cooling air and breathed deeply.

Tomorrow, she would return. She would show up. She would do the work.

But she would do it differently now—no longer confusing endurance with faithfulness, no longer mistaking silence for care.

She was still the one who stayed.

But she was no longer staying unconsciously.

And that awareness, she knew, would not let her go back to who she had been.

Whatever came next would require something new.

Something truer.

And for the first time, Miriam trusted herself to bear that, too.

The praise did not stop.

If anything, it intensified.

In meetings, Miriam's steadiness was invoked as reassurance. In conversations with denominational leaders, her longevity was cited as evidence that the system worked. When new initiatives faltered, someone inevitably said, "Miriam will help us think this through."

She did help.

She also noticed how rarely anyone asked whether she should.

One afternoon, a crisis arose in a neighboring region. It was not technically Miriam's responsibility, but she was asked to advise anyway. The request came framed as respect, even honor.

"You have such perspective," the email said. "We trust your judgment."

Miriam stared at the screen longer than usual.

She felt the familiar pull—the sense that saying no would feel like abandonment, that her absence would leave others exposed. She also felt something new: a clear awareness of what saying yes would require.

She would listen carefully. She would translate complexity into survivable language. She would help the system absorb shock without changing its structure.

She would carry it.

Miriam closed her laptop without responding.

She went for a walk instead, something she had learned to do when decisions felt morally dense. The neighborhood was quiet, the afternoon light gentle. She noticed how her body responded to the possibility of refusal—a mixture of fear and relief.

Halfway down the block, she stopped and sat on a low stone wall.

She realized that much of her staying had been motivated by a fear she had never named: If I don't hold this, it will fall apart.

The belief had felt virtuous. Necessary. Now it felt heavy.

That evening, she drafted a reply.

Thank you for thinking of me, she wrote. I'm not able to take this on right now. I trust the team will find the wisdom they need.

She read it twice, then sent it.

The response came quickly. It was polite. Understanding. No pushback.

And yet, Miriam felt the tremor of having stepped outside a role she had inhabited for years.

The next week, she noticed subtle changes. She was still invited to meetings, but no longer automatically looped into everything. Decisions were made without her input. Occasionally, outcomes were messier.

The system did not collapse.

This surprised her more than she expected.

In one meeting, a colleague struggled visibly with a decision Miriam would once have navigated smoothly. The room grew tense. Someone looked toward her instinctively, then stopped.

Miriam remained silent.

The colleague found his footing slowly, awkwardly. The conversation took longer. The outcome was less polished.

But something else happened too.

Responsibility redistributed.

Afterward, the colleague approached her. "That was hard," he said. "But I think it was good for me."

Miriam nodded. "I think so too."

She felt a strange mix of grief and relief. She had spent years protecting others from discomfort. Now she was watching them grow into it.

At home that evening, Miriam returned to her notebook.

Staying taught me how to carry, she wrote.

Letting go is teaching me how to trust.

The words felt true.

Still, there were moments when doubt surfaced. When a decision went poorly. When someone was hurt in ways she might have prevented. The old reflex surged then, urging her to reinsert herself, to resume the work of quiet correction.

She resisted—not out of indifference, but out of conviction.

She was learning that presence did not have to mean absorption.

One afternoon, she met with the younger colleague who had first asked the difficult question months earlier. They spoke candidly about the changes unfolding.

"I've noticed you're stepping back more," the colleague said carefully. "Are you okay?"

Miriam smiled. "I'm learning," she said. "How not to confuse usefulness with faithfulness."

The colleague nodded slowly. "That's. . . not something we talk about much."

"No," Miriam agreed. "But we should."

As the months passed, Miriam felt something in her begin to expand—not dramatically, not publicly. She found herself thinking more freely, imagining possibilities she had long dismissed as unrealistic.

She did not yet know whether she would leave. That question remained open, unresolved. But staying no longer felt like a closed system.

It felt like a choice she could revisit without self-betrayal.

One evening, after a long day, Miriam sat alone in her office and looked around the room she had occupied for so many years. The shelves bore the marks of time—binders labeled in her handwriting, framed photos of long-past gatherings.

She felt affection. Gratitude. Weariness.

She also felt something she had not expected.

Agency.

Not the power to control outcomes. Not the authority to decide everything. But the freedom to decide what she would and would not carry.

She turned off the light and closed the door behind her.

The hallway was quiet. The building steady.

For the first time in a long while, Miriam did not feel responsible for holding it all together.

She had stayed.

She was still staying.

But she was no longer disappearing in the process.

And that—she sensed—might be the most faithful thing she had done in years.

Miriam did not leave.

That surprised people more than if she had.

After the shift—after the questions, the refusals, the moments when she stopped absorbing what others avoided—many assumed departure was inevitable. They spoke to her with a new tone, careful and anticipatory, as if bracing for an announcement.

None came.

What changed instead was quieter, harder to narrate.

Miriam remained in the system, but she was no longer shaped by its reflexes. She attended meetings without preemptively translating. She spoke less often, but more plainly. She allowed pauses to linger. She let decisions be imperfect when perfection depended on her self-erasure.

The system adjusted around her.

Not dramatically. Not cleanly. But unmistakably.

Some colleagues leaned in. Others pulled back. A few grew wary, unsure whether Miriam would still do the invisible work she had once done without complaint.

She no longer did.

One afternoon, a senior leader stopped by her office. The conversation was polite, meandering at first, then carefully direct.

"We've noticed a change," he said.

Miriam nodded. "I imagine you have."

"We just want to make sure everything's okay," he continued. "You've always been such a stabilizing presence."

Miriam felt the old language hover between them, familiar and tempting.

"I'm still committed," she said calmly. "I'm just no longer willing to be the place where unresolved tension gets stored."

The leader frowned slightly—not offended, but unsettled.

"That's. . . an interesting way to put it," he said.

"It's an accurate one," Miriam replied.

The conversation ended without conflict, but not without consequence. Miriam knew she had named something that could not be unnamed.

Walking home that evening, she reflected on how far she had come without ever leaving her post. She had not escaped the system. She had changed her posture within it.

That felt more dangerous than departure.

Leaving would have resolved the discomfort quickly. Staying differently allowed the discomfort to remain distributed—visible, shared, harder to manage.

In the months that followed, Miriam noticed how often others began to name cost more directly. A colleague spoke openly about moral fatigue. Another admitted uncertainty without immediately softening it. The language of endurance slowly lost some of its shine.

Not because Miriam demanded it.

Because she stopped performing it.

One evening, she met again with the younger leader she mentored. They sat together after a long day, the building nearly empty.

"I've been thinking about that question I asked you," the younger woman said. "About when staying becomes harmful."

Miriam smiled faintly. "I have too."

"I think I used to believe that staying was always the braver choice," the woman continued. "Now I'm not so sure."

"Bravery isn't about duration," Miriam said. "It's about honesty."

The woman nodded, eyes thoughtful. "Do you think you'll ever leave?"

Miriam considered the question carefully.

"Yes," she said finally. "Probably."

"And?"

"And I don't feel rushed," Miriam added. "For the first time, staying doesn't feel like avoidance. It feels like discernment."

That distinction mattered more than any plan.

As the year turned, Miriam felt a steadiness return—not the old steadiness that came from containment, but something looser, more alive. She laughed more easily. She slept better. She noticed when resentment arose and addressed it instead of folding it inward.

She had not become reckless.

She had become available to herself.

At a retreat near the end of the year, Miriam was invited to reflect publicly on longevity in leadership. She stood at the front of the room, facing colleagues who had known her for decades.

"I've been here a long time," she began. "And for many years, I thought staying meant protecting the institution from discomfort."

The room was quiet.

"I'm learning," she continued, "that staying can also mean refusing to absorb what should be faced together."

She paused, letting the words settle.

"Longevity doesn't make us faithful by default," she said. "Faithfulness requires that we remain morally present—not just physically present."

No one applauded. No one argued.

The silence felt different now—less constricting, more receptive.

Later that night, alone in her room, Miriam sat by the window and looked out at the darkened grounds. She felt the accumulated weight of her years settle into something like coherence—not resolution, but alignment.

She thought about all the times she had told herself she stayed for others.

That had been true.

What she knew now was that staying also required something from her—and that she no longer had to pay that cost invisibly.

Miriam did not know how long she would remain where she was. She did not need to.

What mattered was that she no longer mistook endurance for virtue, or continuity for care.

She had stayed long enough to know what staying could cost.

Now she was staying with her eyes open.

And that—quietly, insistently—had begun to change not only her, but the space around her.

She locked her office door for the night and walked down the hallway, her footsteps unhurried.

The building was steady.

So was she.

Not because she had learned how to carry everything.

But because she had finally learned what she no longer would.

STORY 8

Still Here on Sunday

ELLEN ARRIVED EARLY, AS she always did.

The parking lot was mostly empty, the morning air cool enough to raise goosebumps on her arms as she stepped out of the car. She paused for a moment before locking the door, listening to the quiet. This was her favorite part of Sunday—the calm before the building filled with voices and expectations.

Inside, the sanctuary smelled faintly of coffee and old wood. Sunlight filtered through the stained glass, casting muted colors across the pews. Ellen slipped into her usual seat, third row from the back on the left, close enough to feel involved, far enough not to be noticed if she needed to sit still.

She set her bulletin neatly beside her and folded her hands in her lap.

She had been sitting in this church for more than twenty years. She knew the rhythms by heart—the rise and fall of the liturgy, the cadence of familiar hymns, the places where silence would come. She knew where the pastor's voice would soften, where it would turn hopeful, where it would avoid certain edges altogether.

That knowledge used to comfort her.

Now, it felt heavier.

As the prelude began, Ellen closed her eyes and breathed slowly. She wanted to arrive fully, to resist the quiet bracing that had become second nature. She had told herself, again this morning, that she was here because she loved this place. Because faith had taken root here. Because leaving would feel like tearing something out by the roots.

The opening hymn was familiar. Ellen sang, her voice steady, though she noticed how carefully she chose which words to emphasize. There were lines she sang easily, lines that caught slightly in her throat. She wondered, not for the first time, when that hesitation had begun.

During the prayer of confession, Ellen bowed her head. The words were gentle, general—sins of distraction, of not loving fully, of failing to trust. She waited for something more specific, something that might name the weight she carried into the pew each week.

It did not come.

She lifted her head at the assurance of pardon, feeling both relieved and oddly unsatisfied. Forgiveness had been declared, but she was not sure what, exactly, had been confessed.

The sermon followed the same careful pattern. The text was challenging—one that had once stirred her deeply. Ellen leaned forward slightly, listening closely, hoping.

The pastor spoke of kindness. Of humility. Of avoiding judgment in divisive times.

Ellen felt a familiar tightening in her chest.

She agreed with what was being said. That, she realized, was part of the problem. The sermon was true—but it was incomplete. It named virtues without naming stakes. It spoke of peace without naming what peace might require.

She glanced around the sanctuary. Heads nodded. Pens moved across sermon notes. A few people murmured assent.

Ellen wondered if anyone else felt the absence she felt, the way something essential hovered just outside the frame of the words.

As the sermon ended, she sat back, her hands clasped tightly now. She felt tired—not bored, not angry, just quietly depleted.

After worship, she lingered near the back, chatting politely with people she had known for years. Conversations were easy. Familiar. Safe.

"Good sermon today," someone said.

"Yes," Ellen replied. "It was."

Another person asked about her week. Someone mentioned an upcoming potluck. The church moved, seamlessly, into its social rhythms.

Ellen smiled, nodded, listened. She had learned how to do this without thinking.

On her way out, she paused by the sanctuary doors and looked back once more at the space. She felt affection rise unexpectedly—gratitude for baptisms remembered, for funerals held with care, for years of shared prayer.

She also felt the weight of what she did not know how to say.

Driving home, Ellen replayed the sermon in her mind. She tried to imagine what it would sound like if the pastor had named the things she found herself thinking about all week—the public witness of the church, the silence around suffering she saw plainly, the cost of always choosing gentleness over truth.

She imagined what it would feel like to raise her hand in adult education and ask a question that could not be answered quickly.

She imagined the room growing quiet.

At a stoplight, Ellen exhaled slowly. She knew why she did not ask those questions. She knew how easily concern could turn into disruption, how quickly honesty could be labeled divisive.

She did not want to be that person.

At home, Ellen set her purse down and sat at the kitchen table, still in her church clothes. She stared out the window at her small backyard, noticing the way the light shifted as clouds passed overhead.

She thought about leaving. The thought came more often now, uninvited but persistent. She knew people who had left—some angrily, some quietly, some with a sense of relief she envied and mistrusted.

Leaving felt too final.

Staying, she was beginning to realize, was not neutral.

That afternoon, Ellen opened her Bible and turned to the text from the sermon. She read it slowly, lingering over phrases that felt sharper on the page than they had from the pulpit. She felt the familiar stirring of conviction—the reason she kept coming back, the reason she stayed.

Faith still mattered to her. The church still mattered.

What she did not know was how much of herself she could continue to bracket in order to remain.

That night, as she prepared for bed, Ellen felt the quiet ache settle in again. It was not dramatic. It did not demand attention.

It simply waited.

On Sunday morning, she would return. She would sit in her pew. She would sing and pray and listen.

She was still here.

What she did not yet know was how long that would be enough—or what it was costing her to stay.

The silence did not begin in worship.

Ellen noticed it first in conversation.

It appeared in the careful way people spoke about the news, referring obliquely to events everyone clearly knew about but no one named directly. It surfaced in Bible study when a question drifted close to politics or power or suffering and was gently redirected back to something safer, more personal.

"Let's remember to focus on what we can control," someone would say.

Ellen learned how to hear that phrase as a boundary marker.

She sat in her usual circle on Wednesday evenings, her Bible open, pen resting unused in her hand. The discussion moved steadily through the passage, highlighting themes of kindness and patience. When someone mentioned justice, the word hung briefly in the air before being folded back into individual behavior.

Ellen felt the now-familiar tightening in her chest.

She wondered how many people in the room felt it too.

At one point, the leader asked, "Does anyone have anything else to add?"

The room was quiet. Ellen's heart beat faster. She felt words rising—measured, careful, not accusatory. She wanted to ask how faith shaped their response to what was happening beyond the walls of the church. She wanted to know how they understood discipleship when harm felt structural rather than personal.

She pictured the faces around the circle. She imagined the polite discomfort, the subtle shift, the way the conversation would likely move on without resolution.

Ellen stayed quiet.

Driving home afterward, she felt a familiar mix of relief and disappointment. Relief that she had not disrupted the group. Disappointment that the disruption might have been necessary.

She wondered when she had learned that protecting harmony mattered more than speaking truth.

The next Sunday, the pattern repeated itself. The service was thoughtful, reverent, measured. The prayers named general concerns—violence, division, uncertainty—without specificity. Ellen bowed her head, feeling gratitude for the care with which the words were chosen and frustration at what they avoided.

She caught herself thinking, If this church ever named what weighs on me, I might not know what to do.

The thought startled her.

After worship, she chatted with a friend she had known for years. They spoke about family, about health, about upcoming travel. Finally, the friend said quietly, "Sometimes I feel like we're not allowed to talk about certain things here."

Ellen looked at her, surprised.

"Yes," she said before she could stop herself. "I feel that too."

The friend exhaled, relief evident. "I thought it was just me."

They stood together for a moment, the recognition tender and unsettling.

"Do you think we should say something?" the friend asked.

Ellen hesitated. "I don't know how," she said honestly. "And I don't know what would happen if we did."

They hugged briefly before parting, neither reassured nor resolved.

That afternoon, Ellen took a walk through her neighborhood, the air crisp and bright. She passed houses she had watched fill and empty over the years, seasons turning without asking permission.

She thought about the word faithfulness. How often she had heard it used to describe consistency, presence, loyalty. She wondered when it had come to mean silence.

Ellen did not think of herself as brave. She did not want to be confrontational. She valued community deeply and understood how fragile it could be.

What troubled her was the growing sense that her silence was no longer neutral.

At home, she pulled out an old journal from years earlier. She flipped through pages filled with prayers, reflections, questions she had once asked freely. The handwriting was looser, more exploratory. The questions were bolder.

She paused at one entry.

If faith doesn't speak to this, what is it for?

She closed the journal, feeling the weight of the question settle in her again.

Over the next weeks, Ellen noticed how often she edited herself—how she chose her words carefully in committee meetings, how she softened comments in class, how she redirected conversations in her own mind before they ever reached her mouth.

She did not feel censored.

She felt trained.

One evening, she attended a community forum at a nearby church—one that spoke more directly about social issues. The room buzzed with energy. The language was sharper, the questions more open.

Ellen felt both drawn in and uneasy.

Driving home afterward, she realized what unsettled her most: not the content, but the freedom with which it was spoken. She imagined bringing that same candor into her own church and felt a flush of anxiety.

It would change things, she thought.

The next Sunday, Ellen arrived early again. She sat in her pew and watched people enter, greeting one another warmly. She felt affection for them—these people who had prayed with her, grieved with her, shown up when it mattered.

She also felt the growing distance between who she was becoming and what could be spoken aloud here.

During the sermon, the pastor referenced "difficult times" without elaboration. Ellen felt something inside her give way—not in anger, but in weariness.

She realized she was tired of translating her faith into something smaller so that it would fit.

As the service ended, Ellen remained seated longer than usual. The sanctuary emptied gradually. She watched people leave, feeling the familiar pull of belonging and the quieter pull of integrity.

She did not yet know what she would do.

She knew only that staying required more than showing up. It required a constant negotiation with herself—a decision, made over and over again, about which parts of her conscience could remain unspoken.

Ellen stood finally and walked slowly toward the door.

She was still here.

But she was beginning to understand that staying was not just an act of loyalty.

It was an act of moral endurance.

And she was no longer sure how long she could keep paying that price without naming it.

The first time Ellen spoke, nothing happened.

That surprised her.

It was during an adult education class, one of the more thoughtful ones—smaller, intentionally conversational. The topic was discipleship in uncertain times, a phrase broad enough to mean almost anything.

The facilitator invited reflections. A few people shared about personal habits, about prayer and resilience. Ellen listened, feeling the familiar pressure build as the conversation hovered near something real and then drifted away.

Before she could think better of it, she raised her hand.

"I keep wondering," she said carefully, "how our faith shapes what we pay attention to—not just personally, but together. What we're willing to name."

The room went quiet.

Not tense. Just still.

The facilitator nodded slowly. "Can you say more?"

Ellen felt her pulse quicken. She had not expected that.

"I guess," she continued, choosing her words with care, "I sometimes feel like we talk around the things that weigh on us most. And I'm not sure whether that's gentleness—or avoidance."

No one spoke for a moment. Ellen felt exposed, aware of her breath, her posture, the sound of her own voice lingering in the air.

Then someone said, "I've felt that too."

Another added, "I didn't know how to put it, but yes."

The conversation shifted—not dramatically, but noticeably. People spoke more slowly. Someone named fear. Someone else named exhaustion. The language remained careful, but it felt closer to the bone.

Ellen felt a cautious relief.

After the class ended, a woman approached her quietly. "Thank you for saying that," she said. "I've been holding it for a long time."

Ellen smiled, surprised by the warmth she felt.

Driving home, she replayed the moment, half-expecting regret to surface. It didn't. What she felt instead was a flicker of possibility.

Maybe, she thought, speaking didn't always have to break things.

The next Sunday, she arrived with that possibility still faintly alive in her. She listened more attentively, noticed more sharply. During the prayers, she felt the familiar frustration rise again at what was left unnamed—but this time, it was accompanied by something else.

Agency.

She wondered what would happen if she asked the pastor for a conversation.

The thought unsettled her.

Ellen had always seen the pastor as kind, thoughtful, careful in ways she appreciated and sometimes resented. She trusted his intentions. She did not trust the system around him to receive certain truths easily.

That afternoon, she sat at her kitchen table with her laptop open, staring at a blank email draft. She typed a sentence, then deleted it. Typed again. Deleted again.

Finally, she wrote simply:

Would you be willing to talk sometime? I've been carrying some questions about how we name what's happening in the world and in our life together.

She hovered over the send button, heart racing.

Then she clicked it.

The reply came later that evening.

Of course. I'm glad you reached out.

Relief washed over her, followed quickly by anxiety.

They met the following week in the pastor's office. The space was familiar, books lining the walls, sunlight filtering in through a small window. Ellen sat across from him, hands folded tightly in her lap.

"I want to be clear," she began. "I'm not angry. And I'm not trying to start conflict."

The pastor smiled gently. "You don't need to preface," he said. "I'm listening."

Ellen took a breath.

"I love this church," she said. "It's my home. And lately, I've been feeling a growing gap between what I believe our faith calls us to name—and what we actually say out loud together."

The pastor nodded slowly.

"I worry," she continued, "that our carefulness is costing us something. That people are carrying things alone because they don't see space to speak."

The pastor was quiet for a long moment.

"I hear that," he said finally. "And I struggle with it too."

Ellen felt a mix of relief and sadness at the admission.

"There are pressures you may not see," he added. "Concerns about unity. About not alienating people."

"I understand that," Ellen said. "I really do. I just don't know how much longer I can keep bracketing parts of my conscience to belong."

The words surprised her with their directness.

The pastor did not flinch. "That's important to say," he replied. "And it's not something I want you to carry alone."

They talked for nearly an hour. Nothing was resolved. No plan was formed. But Ellen left feeling lighter—not because the church had changed, but because she had been honest.

In the weeks that followed, Ellen noticed subtle shifts in herself. She spoke a little more freely in small groups. She named discomfort without apology. Sometimes the room met her with openness. Sometimes with silence.

Both were easier to bear than self-erasure.

Still, the cost of staying remained.

There were Sundays when the sermon avoided what she longed to hear. Prayers that circled rather than named. Conversations that retreated just when they became interesting.

Ellen felt the ache of that absence more sharply now that she had tasted something else.

One evening, she sat with her journal open, writing without intention. Words came slowly.

I am still here, she wrote.

But I am no longer invisible to myself.

The sentence felt like a threshold.

Ellen did not know where this path would lead. She did not know whether staying would remain possible, or whether honesty would eventually push her to the margins—or out entirely.

What she knew was this: staying was no longer passive.

It required discernment. Courage. A willingness to risk small ruptures rather than live with constant internal division.

The next Sunday, she arrived early again and took her seat. The sanctuary filled gradually, familiar faces settling into familiar places.

As the prelude began, Ellen closed her eyes and breathed deeply.

She was still here.

But now, she was here with her eyes open.

And that, she sensed, would change what staying meant—whatever came next.

Ellen began to notice how staying changed her body before it changed her mind.

It showed up as tension she could not quite release during worship, a subtle bracing when certain phrases were spoken, a shallow breath she only realized she was holding when the service ended. These were not dramatic reactions. No one would have noticed them from the outside.

But she noticed.

One Sunday, during the passing of the peace, a man she had known for years clasped her hands warmly and said, "It's good to see you. This place feels like an anchor right now."

Ellen smiled. "It does," she said, meaning both yes and no at once.

She felt the now-familiar split inside her—gratitude for the steadiness the church offered, and grief for the narrowing she felt required to remain part of it.

The sermon that day came close. So close.

The text dealt with truth and courage, with the cost of discipleship. Ellen leaned forward as the pastor spoke, feeling her heart quicken. There were moments when she was sure the sermon would cross the threshold, would finally name the things she felt everyone carrying just beneath the surface.

But each time, the language softened. The edge was rounded off. Courage became inward. Cost became personal inconvenience.

When the sermon ended, Ellen felt the familiar hollow settle in her chest.

She did not blame the pastor. That surprised her.

She had stopped imagining this as a failure of character or courage. She understood now that it was structural—a web of expectations, fears, and unspoken agreements that shaped what could be said without consequence.

That understanding made it harder, not easier.

After worship, Ellen found herself lingering in the sanctuary long after most people had left. She watched the ushers stack bulletins, the choir members chatting quietly as they gathered their things. The space felt tender in its ordinariness.

She wondered how many people carried what she carried.

Later that week, Ellen met with her friend—the one who had once admitted feeling the same quiet constraint. They sat together over coffee, the conversation easy at first, then deeper.

"I almost said something last Sunday," the friend admitted. "During the prayers."

"What stopped you?" Ellen asked.

The friend shrugged. "I didn't want to make things awkward."

Ellen nodded. "I know that feeling."

They sat in silence for a moment.

"I keep asking myself," the friend continued, "whether staying is making me more faithful—or just more careful."

The question hung between them, weighty and unresolved.

Ellen realized then that staying had become an ongoing moral calculation. Each Sunday, each meeting, each conversation required a quiet discernment: Is this a moment to speak—or a moment to hold?

She had grown skilled at that discernment.

She was also growing tired of it.

One evening, Ellen attended a vigil downtown after a public tragedy. People gathered in the cold, holding candles, speaking names, naming grief plainly. The prayers were raw, unpolished, sometimes halting.

Ellen felt something inside her loosen.

Driving home afterward, she wondered why that kind of naming felt possible here but not in her church. She wondered what the difference was—and what it said about the space she returned to each Sunday.

The next morning, she woke with an unexpected clarity.

She was not angry at her church.

She was grieving it.

Grieving what it had been when she first arrived—when faith felt expansive, when questions were welcomed, when silence was not mistaken for unity. Grieving the version of herself who had once spoken freely without calculating impact.

Grief, she realized, explained the ache better than frustration ever had.

That Sunday, as she sat in her pew, Ellen allowed herself to feel it fully. She sang with a steadiness that surprised her, her voice clear and unguarded. During the prayers, she bowed her head and named silently what was missing, what was longed for, what felt unfinished.

She did not rush herself toward a decision.

After worship, the pastor greeted her warmly and asked how she was doing.

Ellen hesitated, then answered honestly. "I'm still here," she said. "And I'm thinking a lot about what that means."

The pastor nodded, not pressing for more. "I'm glad you're here," he said.

Ellen believed him.

That evening, she sat at her kitchen table again, the familiar place of reflection. She opened her journal and wrote slowly.

Staying is not the absence of injury, she wrote.

Sometimes it is where injury learns to be quiet.

She paused, then added another line.

The question is not whether I can endure this.

The question is whether I am allowed to remain whole.

The words felt steady, not accusatory.

Ellen knew she had not reached a conclusion. She did not know whether she would eventually leave, or whether the church would change in ways she could not yet see. She did not know whether her honesty would find more room—or whether it would slowly isolate her.

What she knew was that staying was no longer unconscious.

It was a choice she made with her eyes open, week after week.

The next Sunday, she arrived early again. The parking lot was quiet, the air cool. She paused before entering, breathing deeply, feeling the weight and the love, the belonging and the cost.

She stepped inside.

She was still here.

And she was beginning to understand that staying, like leaving, carried moral weight—weight that could not be dismissed, only borne with honesty.

For now, she chose to stay.

Not because it was easy.

But because she was not yet ready to give up on the possibility that a place she loved could learn to speak again.

Whether that hope would hold, she did not know.

But she would not pretend anymore that staying was painless.

She took her seat, folded her hands, and waited—not for resolution, but for truth, wherever it might finally find voice.

The cost of staying did not announce itself all at once.

It accumulated quietly, like sediment.

Ellen noticed it in the way Sundays now lingered into Monday. She would leave worship and move through the rest of the day carrying a low-grade heaviness she could not easily set down. By Monday morning, she often felt strangely depleted—not because anything difficult had happened, but because something essential had not.

She began to recognize the pattern.

On weeks when worship came close to naming what mattered, she felt energized, even if unresolved. On weeks when everything stayed careful and smooth, she felt dull and distant, as though she had participated in something incomplete.

The incompleteness was exhausting.

One Sunday, during communion, Ellen stood in line with the others, hands folded, eyes lowered. The words were spoken gently: The body of Christ, given for you.

She felt the familiar swell of gratitude—and then, unexpectedly, a flash of grief.

She wondered what it meant to receive a body that bore wounds while belonging to a community so hesitant to name its own.

Back in her pew, she closed her eyes and felt tears rise without clear cause. She wiped them away quickly, hoping no one noticed.

After worship, she declined an invitation to lunch with friends, citing errands. She drove instead to a nearby park and sat on a bench, letting the quiet settle around her.

She felt tired—not of people, not of faith, but of holding her tongue.

Ellen realized that staying required a constant internal sorting: What can I say here? What must I keep to myself? Over time, that sorting had begun to shape not just her speech, but her imagination. She found herself thinking smaller thoughts, asking safer questions, anticipating limits before encountering them.

She wondered how much of herself had already adjusted.

That afternoon, she pulled out the journal again, the one that had begun to feel like her most honest companion. She wrote slowly, deliberately.

Staying has taught me how to belong without being fully known, she wrote.

I'm not sure how long a soul can live like that.

The words startled her. She had not planned to write them.

Over the next weeks, Ellen experimented with small acts of honesty. She asked slightly sharper questions in class. She named discomfort without apology. Sometimes the room met her with curiosity. Other times with silence that felt heavier than disagreement.

She learned to tolerate both.

Still, the emotional cost mounted.

One evening, she found herself snapping at her partner over something trivial. The reaction surprised her with its intensity. Later, as she lay awake, she traced the irritation back—not to the argument itself, but to the accumulated effort of restraint she carried into the rest of her life.

She began to understand that unspoken truth does not disappear.

It leaks.

At the next session meeting open to congregants, Ellen sat quietly in the back, listening as leaders discussed attendance trends and financial stability. The conversation was competent, forward-looking. She admired their care.

When public witness came up briefly, it was framed cautiously—how to remain welcoming, how to avoid polarization.

Ellen felt the now-familiar tightening.

She imagined raising her hand and asking, What are we afraid of losing if we speak more clearly? She imagined the room stiffening, the careful explanations that would follow.

She did not raise her hand.

Driving home afterward, she felt a sharp clarity cut through her usual ambivalence.

This is hurting me, she thought.

Not in a way anyone would recognize as harm. Not enough to justify dramatic action. But enough to be real.

She realized then that moral injury did not require catastrophe.

It required prolonged dissonance.

That night, Ellen talked with her partner more openly than she had before.

"I don't know how to stay without becoming smaller," she said quietly.

Her partner listened, then asked gently, "What would it look like to stay without shrinking?"

Ellen had no immediate answer.

The question stayed with her.

Over the following Sundays, Ellen noticed herself watching newcomers more closely—wondering what they sensed, what they felt, how quickly they learned what could and could not be spoken. She wondered what kind of formation was happening beneath the surface of politeness and warmth.

She wondered what kind of formation she herself was undergoing.

One morning, as she arrived early again and took her seat, Ellen felt a deep affection for the sanctuary, for the light filtering through the windows, for the familiarity that had held her through seasons of life.

She also felt the ache of knowing that love did not negate cost.

As the service began, she breathed deeply and made a quiet decision—not about leaving or staying, but about honesty.

She would stop pretending that this was painless.

She would stop minimizing what it took to be here.

She did not yet know what that would require or where it would lead. She only knew that her faith could not survive indefinite silence without consequence.

After worship, as she stood chatting near the door, someone asked casually, "How long have you been here now?"

Ellen smiled. "A long time," she said.

"And you're still here," the person added warmly.

"Yes," Ellen replied. "I am."

The words landed differently now.

Still here did not mean untouched.

Still here did not mean whole.

It meant choosing, again and again, to remain in a space that shaped her—for better and for harm.

Ellen stepped outside into the cool air and paused on the steps, letting the door close softly behind her. She felt the familiar mixture of love and grief settle into her chest.

She did not yet know how the story would end.

What she knew was this: staying had become a morally serious act—one that required truthfulness, courage, and care not only for the community she loved, but for herself.

For now, she stayed.

But she would no longer pretend that staying was free.

The weight she carried was real.

And naming that weight, at last, felt like the beginning of something—whatever came next.

The decision did not arrive as a conclusion.

It came as a shift in how Ellen carried herself through the door each Sunday.

She noticed it first in her body. The bracing softened—not because the silence had disappeared, but because she had stopped pretending it wasn't there. She no longer entered worship hoping the service would finally say what she needed it to say. She entered attentive instead, listening for what was named and for what remained absent, without trying to make either mean more than it did.

This did not make Sundays easier.

It made them clearer.

One morning, during the prayers of the people, the congregation paused for spoken requests. A long silence followed. Ellen felt the familiar urge to fill it—to name something specific, something heavy, something undeniably real.

Her heart beat faster.

She imagined the words she could speak. She imagined the room absorbing them awkwardly, perhaps gratefully, perhaps not. She imagined the looks afterward, the conversations that might follow.

She also imagined the relief of not carrying the words alone anymore.

Ellen opened her mouth.

Then she closed it again.

Not because she was afraid.

Because she realized something important: speaking once would not undo a culture of silence. And she did not want her honesty to become a moment others could point to and say, See? We allow that.

She wanted more than permission.

She wanted shared responsibility.

The silence ended when the pastor offered a concluding prayer. Worship moved on.

Ellen sat quietly, not angry with herself, not triumphant either. She felt steady.

After the service, she stayed behind and helped stack chairs, moving slowly, deliberately. A woman she barely knew struck up a conversation, then hesitated.

"I don't know how to say this," the woman said finally, "but sometimes I feel like we're holding our breath in here."

Ellen looked at her, startled and grateful.

"Yes," she said simply. "I feel that too."

They stood together for a moment, the sanctuary nearly empty now.

"I don't know what to do about it," the woman added.

"Neither do I," Ellen replied. "But I think noticing it matters."

The woman nodded, eyes bright, then thanked her and left.

Ellen felt the exchange echo inside her—not as resolution, but as confirmation. She was not alone. She had never been alone. She had simply been quiet alongside others who were also quiet.

Driving home, Ellen realized that something fundamental had changed. She no longer experienced herself as a solitary dissenter enduring a collective denial. She saw now how silence had been shared, even if unacknowledged.

That recognition brought both comfort and sorrow.

Over the following weeks, Ellen stopped framing her discernment as a binary choice between staying and leaving. She began to ask different questions instead.

What kind of presence can I offer without disappearing?

What truths can I name without carrying them alone?

What does faithfulness look like when the community is not ready to follow?

These questions did not yield immediate answers.

But they gave her a way to live honestly in the meantime.

She spoke when she could. She stayed quiet when she needed to. She refused to smooth over her own discomfort for the sake of appearing agreeable. When conversations stalled, she let them stall.

She also began to grieve more openly—not publicly, but internally. She allowed herself to feel the sadness of loving a church that could not yet love the truth she longed to speak.

Grief, she discovered, was less corrosive than resentment.

One evening, Ellen sat again at her kitchen table, journal open, the familiar place where things finally came into focus. She wrote slowly.

I am still here, she wrote.

But I am no longer confusing presence with consent.

The sentence felt like a line she could live by.

Months passed. Nothing dramatic happened. The church did not suddenly change course. The sermons remained careful. The prayers remained broad. The culture remained polite, restrained, kind.

And yet.

Ellen noticed more people pausing before answering questions. More silences lingering a moment longer than before. More quiet admissions offered one-on-one, in hallways, over coffee.

The silence was still there.

But it was thinner.

One Sunday morning, Ellen arrived early again, the parking lot mostly empty, the air cool. She paused before locking her car, just as she always did.

This time, she noticed something new.

She did not feel braced.

She felt attentive.

Inside, the sanctuary glowed softly in the early light. Ellen took her seat and folded her hands. She felt the familiar love, the familiar ache, the familiar hope.

All of it together.

She knew she might still leave someday. That possibility remained real and unresolved. Staying was no longer a lifetime promise, nor was leaving a failure.

What mattered now was that she no longer betrayed herself in order to belong.

As the prelude began, Ellen closed her eyes and breathed deeply.

She was still here.

Not because it was easy.

Not because it was painless.

But because she was choosing to remain present—to herself, to her faith, to the truth as she understood it—without demanding that the church be something it was not yet ready to be.

Staying, she now understood, was not the opposite of courage.

Sometimes, it was its quietest form.

And sometimes, courage meant staying long enough to name the cost—without insisting that it be repaid.

Ellen opened her eyes as the service began.

She sang.

She listened.

She noticed.

She remained.

And whatever came next—whether departure or deeper belonging—she knew she would not meet it by disappearing.

She would meet it whole.
Still here.
And finally honest about what that meant.

STORY 9

What Couldn't Be Fixed

JONAH HAD LEARNED HOW to sit still.

That was the first skill pastoral care had taught him—not how to speak, not how to pray, but how to remain in a room without reaching for relief. He had learned how to let silence stretch without filling it, how to keep his face open when the story being told had no clear edge.

Still, there were limits to that skill.

He felt them now, sitting across from Claire in the small conference room that had become their regular meeting place. The room was plain: a table, two chairs, a window that looked out onto the parking lot. Nothing about it suggested intimacy or safety. And yet, this was where Claire had chosen to speak.

She sat with her hands wrapped tightly around a mug that had long since gone cold. Her posture was careful, as if she were holding herself together through sheer concentration.

"I don't think there's anything left to try," she said quietly.

Jonah did not respond right away. He felt the familiar reflex stir in him—the urge to ask clarifying questions, to identify next steps, to offer options that might reintroduce movement.

He resisted it.

"Say more," he said instead.

Claire's mouth tightened slightly. "I've done everything they asked," she continued. "Every meeting. Every mediation. Every pause for discernment. I've apologized where they wanted apologies. I've been patient when they said patience was faithful."

Her voice wavered, then steadied.

"And it hasn't changed what happened. It's just. . . stretched it out."

Jonah nodded slowly. He felt the truth of her words land in his body. He had seen this pattern before—the slow prolonging of harm in the name of care, the belief that time itself could heal what had been morally ruptured.

"What feels most unbearable right now?" he asked.

Claire looked at him, her eyes sharp with something like disbelief.

"That everyone keeps asking me what I'm going to do next," she said. "As if the right decision will make this okay."

Jonah felt the weight of that land. He knew the question well. He had asked it himself in earlier seasons, believing it to be responsible, hopeful, necessary.

"What do you want to do next?" she continued, her voice rising slightly. "Quit? Stay? Heal? Forgive? Move on?"

She shook her head. "None of that touches what actually happened."

The silence that followed was heavy, but not empty.

Jonah noticed his own discomfort surface—not with Claire's pain, but with its irreducibility. There was nothing he could offer that would restore what had been lost. No reframing that would honor the truth without diminishing it.

He felt useless.

That, he was learning, was often the truest place to begin.

"I keep thinking," Claire said after a moment, "that if I could just explain it better, someone would finally understand. But the more I talk, the smaller it gets."

Jonah recognized that too—the way language can betray experience when it is forced to serve resolution rather than truth.

"You're not failing at explaining," he said carefully. "You're describing something that doesn't fit the categories they're offering."

Claire laughed softly, without humor. "That's exactly it."

She stared at the table for a moment. "Everyone wants this to be fixable," she said. "Including me. Especially me."

Jonah leaned back slightly, grounding himself. He felt the pull of urgency—the institutional timelines hovering in the background, the unspoken expectation that care should produce outcomes.

He chose his words deliberately.

"What if it isn't fixable?" he asked gently.

Claire looked up sharply.

"I don't mean that as despair," he continued quickly. "I mean it as honesty. What if what you're carrying doesn't resolve into a next step—but still deserves care?"

The room felt charged now, the air thick with something unnamed.

Claire swallowed. "No one's said that to me," she whispered.

Jonah felt a familiar ache in his chest. He knew why. Saying such a thing disrupted too many scripts. It threatened the assumption that time, effort, and good intentions would eventually make everything whole.

He had believed that once.

"How does it feel to hear it?" he asked.

Claire closed her eyes briefly. When she opened them, tears spilled over, uncontained.

"It feels like relief," she said. "And grief."

Jonah nodded. "That makes sense."

They sat together in that space, neither moving to end it. Jonah felt the temptation to offer comfort that would soften the edges, to promise that something good would come of this pain.

He did not.

Instead, he stayed.

After a long while, Claire wiped her eyes and took a breath. "Everyone keeps telling me I need to decide," she said. "But deciding feels like choosing which part of myself to abandon."

Jonah felt the moral clarity of that statement resonate deeply.

"Sometimes," he said slowly, "the most faithful thing isn't deciding. It's refusing to pretend the choice is clean."

Claire considered this, nodding faintly.

"I don't know how to live like this," she admitted. "In the not-knowing."

Jonah felt the urge to reassure her rise instinctively. He resisted it.

"You don't have to know how," he said instead. "You just have to not be alone in it."

The words felt fragile, almost inadequate. And yet, they were the truest thing he could offer.

As the meeting drew to a close, Claire gathered her things slowly. She did not look lighter. She did not look healed.

But something in her posture had shifted—subtly, but unmistakably.

At the door, she turned back to Jonah. "Thank you," she said. "For not trying to make this better."

Jonah nodded, feeling the weight of what she had entrusted to him settle fully now.

After she left, he remained seated, staring at the empty chair across from him. He felt the familiar internal reckoning begin—the quiet fear that he was failing his role by not producing movement, not offering solutions.

He knew the questions that would follow. From supervisors. From the institution. From himself.

What's the plan?

What's the goal?

How are we helping her move forward?

He closed his eyes briefly.

What he had offered today was not progress.

It was presence.

And he knew, with a clarity that unsettled him, that presence might be all that was faithful here—even if it would never be enough for the system that surrounded them.

Jonah gathered his notes slowly, feeling the moral weight settle into place.

This was not a case that could be fixed.

This was a truth that needed to be borne.

And he was no longer sure how long he would be allowed to stay with it—by others, or by himself.

Jonah left the building later than he intended.

The parking lot was nearly empty, the light already fading. He sat in his car for a moment before starting the engine, hands resting on the steering wheel, feeling the residue of the conversation settle into him.

He was accustomed to carrying other people's pain. That was not new.

What unsettled him was how little he had done.

No plan.

No timeline.

No actionable summary he could offer to anyone who might ask.

Just presence.

He knew how that would sound if he said it out loud.

At the next supervision meeting, Jonah listened as colleagues reviewed their cases. There was the familiar language of movement and resolution: progress made, steps taken, clarity emerging. When it was his turn, he spoke carefully.

"Claire is still discerning," he said. "What's most important right now is that she's not being rushed into a decision that would cost her integrity."

The supervisor nodded, then asked, "What's the goal?"

Jonah felt the question land sharply.

"To make sure she's supported," he replied. "To make sure we don't replicate the harm by demanding closure."

The supervisor leaned back slightly. "That's important," she said. "But at some point, she'll need to move forward."

Jonah nodded. "I know."

What he did not say was that forward was not a direction Claire could recognize anymore.

After the meeting, Jonah felt the familiar unease creep in. He replayed the exchange in his mind, wondering whether he had failed to frame the situation responsibly. He knew the pressures his supervisor faced—accountability, consistency, the need to demonstrate that care produced outcomes.

He shared those values.

He also knew, now, that those values had limits.

That afternoon, Jonah reviewed Claire's file again. The notes documented months of careful process: meetings attended, mediations attempted, accommodations offered. On paper, the system had done everything right.

And yet.

The harm persisted.

Not because of neglect, but because the original injury had never been named as such. It had been reframed, softened, proceduralized until it no longer resembled the experience Claire described.

Jonah closed the file.

He realized then that part of what troubled him was how easily his role could become complicit in that same dynamic—translating moral pain into manageable categories, offering care that made the injury more tolerable without honoring its truth.

He had done that before.

The next time he met with Claire, she looked more tired than he remembered. Not fragile, but worn in a way that spoke of ongoing effort.

"They keep asking if I'm ready to decide," she said quietly. "I don't know how to explain that deciding feels like agreeing to a story that isn't true."

Jonah nodded. "You don't have to agree to a false story," he said.

Claire looked at him searchingly. "But they need one," she said. "Don't they?"

Jonah hesitated. He felt the familiar tension rise—the desire to reassure her that honesty would be welcomed, that truth would be held.

He did not believe that.

"They need one," he said honestly. "But you don't have to provide it."

Claire exhaled slowly, a mix of relief and fear crossing her face.

"What happens if I don't?" she asked.

Jonah felt the weight of that question press against his chest. He knew the institutional answer. He also knew it was insufficient.

"What happens," he said carefully, "is that the discomfort shifts. It stops living entirely inside you."

They sat with that for a moment.

"I'm afraid," Claire admitted. "If I don't move, I'll be seen as the problem."

Jonah nodded. "That's a real risk."

The honesty felt stark, but necessary.

"What I can promise," he continued, "is that I won't turn your pain into a problem to be solved."

Claire's eyes filled again, though she did not cry.

"That matters," she said.

After she left, Jonah felt the familiar reckoning return. He knew he was offering something fragile—care that could not be measured, progress that could not be demonstrated.

He also knew that refusing to do so would be easier.

That evening, Jonah received an email requesting an update. The language was polite, neutral, expectant.

He stared at the screen, fingers hovering over the keyboard.

He could write what was expected. He could frame Claire's situation as moving slowly toward resolution, emphasize resilience, highlight discernment.

Instead, he wrote this:

Claire is still carrying significant moral pain. What seems most important right now is that we do not rush her into decisions that would require her to minimize or reinterpret what happened. Continued presence and patience are essential.

He read it twice, then sent it.

The reply came the next morning.

Thank you. Let's keep checking in on next steps.

Jonah closed his laptop, feeling both relief and unease. He knew how the system worked. Patience had a shelf life.

Later that week, Jonah sat alone in the sanctuary after hours, the lights dim, the space quiet. He found himself thinking not just about Claire, but about his own formation—how often he had been rewarded for being helpful, efficient, solution-oriented.

He wondered when care had become synonymous with fixing.

He remembered something an old mentor once said: Some wounds don't heal. They teach.

Jonah had nodded at the time, not fully understanding.

Now he did.

The work he was being asked to do with Claire did not feel heroic. It felt exposed. It required him to tolerate scrutiny without the protection of results.

He wondered how long he would be able to do that without pressure to conform.

As he stood to leave, Jonah felt a quiet resolve settle in—not confidence, not certainty, but commitment.

If he was going to fail, he would fail on the side of honoring what could not be fixed.

He did not know what that would cost him.

But he knew what it would cost Claire if he didn't.

And for now, that was enough to guide him—even as the path ahead remained unresolved, unfixable, and morally real.

Pressure arrived quietly.

Not as accusation. Not as demand. As concern.

Jonah felt it in the tone of emails that asked for "updates," in meetings where Claire's name surfaced with a faint impatience, in the subtle shift from curiosity to expectation. He knew this terrain well. Care was welcome as long as it moved things along. Presence was tolerated until it began to slow the machinery.

He had learned how to read those signals early in his work.

"What's the trajectory?" someone asked in passing one afternoon, as if the word itself could summon momentum.

Jonah answered carefully. "She's still living inside the impact. Pushing her toward a narrative of resolution would do more harm."

The colleague nodded, sympathetic. "Of course. We just don't want her to get stuck."

The word lodged in Jonah's chest.

Stuck.

It implied pathology. Resistance. Failure to adapt. It turned endurance into deficiency.

Later that day, Jonah met with Claire again. She looked different this time—not more distressed, but sharper. More alert.

"I think they're getting tired of me," she said.

Jonah did not pretend otherwise. "They're uncomfortable with the waiting," he said. "That doesn't mean you're doing something wrong."

Claire laughed softly. "It feels like it does."

She leaned forward. "I keep wondering if I should just pick an option. Any option. Just to make it stop."

Jonah felt the urgency flare between them. He knew how seductive that impulse was. He had seen it lead people into choices that looked decisive and felt like betrayal months later.

"What would it cost you to do that?" he asked.

Claire did not hesitate. "My credibility with myself."

The clarity of her answer startled him.

They sat with it, letting the words settle.

"I don't think I can survive that," she added quietly.

Jonah nodded. "I believe you."

That belief felt like an act of resistance.

As weeks passed, the pressure intensified. Jonah was asked to summarize the situation more "concretely." He was encouraged to help Claire "move toward acceptance." Someone suggested reframing the experience as growth.

He recognized the pattern.

When harm cannot be repaired, it is often spiritualized.

Jonah resisted the language carefully. He did not accuse. He did not grandstand. He named what he could and refused what he could not.

Still, the strain accumulated.

One evening, Jonah sat at his desk long after the building had emptied, staring at a half-written report. He knew what was expected. He also knew what would be lost if he complied.

He thought about how easily care could become coercive when resolution was treated as the measure of success.

He closed the document without saving.

The next time he met with Claire, she brought something new.

"I think I understand now why this hurts so much," she said.

Jonah waited.

"It's not just what happened," she continued. "It's that everyone wants me to translate it into something manageable. Something that fits."

She shook her head. "I don't want my pain to become instructive. Or inspirational. Or tidy."

Jonah felt the truth of that settle deeply.

"You don't owe anyone that," he said.

Claire looked at him, searching. "Do you ever worry," she asked, "that staying with me like this will cost you?"

The question surprised him with its care.

"Yes," he said honestly.

She nodded. "I thought so."

They sat quietly for a moment.

"Thank you anyway," she said.

That night, Jonah dreamed of standing in a room with no exits, walls lined with files. Each file bore a name. Each name carried a story that did not end. He woke unsettled, the weight of accumulated witness pressing on him.

He realized then that he was not just accompanying Claire. He was confronting the limits of his vocation.

The system could tolerate pain.

It could not tolerate unresolved pain.

At the next supervisory check-in, the question came plainly.

"How much longer do you think this can go on?" his supervisor asked.

Jonah chose his words carefully. "As long as it needs to," he said. "Or until I'm told I can't continue this way."

The supervisor sighed. "We have to think about sustainability."

Jonah nodded. "So do I."

What he did not say was that sustainability, as they defined it, required someone to absorb the cost.

And that someone was almost always the one already injured.

After the meeting, Jonah felt the familiar doubt creep in. Was he enabling avoidance? Was he colluding with stagnation? Was he mistaking restraint for courage?

He returned to Claire's words: I can't survive losing credibility with myself.

That felt like a compass.

The next time someone suggested a timeline, Jonah said simply, "I won't impose one."

The conversation cooled after that.

Weeks later, Claire told him she had made a decision—not about staying or leaving, but about boundaries.

"I've stopped answering certain questions," she said. "The ones that try to push me into a story I don't recognize."

Jonah smiled faintly. "How does that feel?"

"Terrifying," she said. "And strangely solid."

He recognized the feeling.

That afternoon, Jonah received notice that his role would be shifting. Reassigned. Not punitive, not explicit. A reallocation of responsibilities "to meet evolving needs."

He understood.

When he told Claire, she was quiet for a long moment.

"I'm sorry," she said finally. "I didn't want this to cost you."

Jonah shook his head. "It didn't cost me," he said. "It clarified things."

They sat together one last time in the familiar room. Nothing was resolved. Nothing was healed.

But something had been honored.

As Claire stood to leave, she paused at the door. "You didn't fix this," she said.

Jonah nodded. "I know."

"You didn't even try," she added, a small smile forming.

He returned it. "I tried to stay."

"That mattered," she said. "More than you know."

After she left, Jonah sat alone, the chair across from him empty again. He felt the ache of unfinished work, of care interrupted by structure.

He also felt something else.

Integrity.

He did not know what the next season would hold, or whether his way of practicing care would be welcome elsewhere. He knew only that some truths could not be made lighter without being diminished.

And some forms of faithfulness looked like staying until staying was no longer allowed.

Jonah gathered his things slowly and turned off the light.

What couldn't be fixed had been carried, if only for a while.

And that, he knew now, was not nothing.

Jonah discovered that absence had a sound.

It was not silence exactly. It was the faint echo left behind when a role was vacated but the need it served remained. In the weeks after his reassignment, he noticed it everywhere—in emails forwarded to him by mistake, in meetings he no longer attended but still shaped indirectly, in the way colleagues spoke around Claire's situation without naming her.

The system had moved on.

Claire had not.

Jonah met her once more, unofficially, at a café near the old office. The choice of place mattered. Neutral ground. No walls that implied authority or outcome. Just two people at a small table, the noise of ordinary life around them.

Claire looked steadier than he expected. Not lighter. More anchored.

"They've stopped checking in," she said without bitterness. "At first, that hurt. Now it feels. . . clarifying."

Jonah nodded. "How so?"

"I know now what kind of care they can offer," she said. "And what they can't."

The sentence held neither accusation nor resignation. It was simply factual.

Jonah felt a complicated mix of grief and relief rise in him. He had spent so much time trying to help institutions stretch beyond their limits. Now he was watching someone adapt—not by shrinking, but by refusing to expect what could not be given.

"What are you carrying now?" he asked.

Claire stirred her coffee slowly. "The same truth," she said. "But it's quieter. Not because it's healed—because I'm not being asked to explain it every week."

Jonah felt that land with weight.

They sat together for a while, neither rushing. Jonah noticed how different this felt from their previous meetings. There was no agenda, no pressure to demonstrate progress. Just presence, stripped of role.

"I used to think," Claire said finally, "that being cared for meant someone would help me make sense of this. Now I think it means someone doesn't force sense onto it."

Jonah smiled faintly. "That's a hard thing to learn."

"Yes," she said. "And a relief."

As they parted, Claire thanked him again—not with urgency, not with apology, but with quiet recognition. Jonah watched her walk away, feeling the familiar ache of unfinished accompaniment.

This time, he let it be.

In the months that followed, Jonah found himself recalibrating his own sense of vocation. Without the role that had defined him, he felt exposed. He noticed how often his identity had been tied to being needed, to being the one who could sit with what others could not.

He missed the work.

He did not miss the pressure to justify it.

He began seeing a therapist himself, something he had postponed for years under the guise of being "fine." In one session, he spoke aloud what had been circling him since Claire.

"I think I believed that if I stayed long enough, something would resolve," he said. "That my presence could eventually tip the balance."

The therapist nodded. "And now?"

"Now I think some systems depend on people like me to absorb what they can't afford to face," Jonah said quietly.

"That's an important recognition," she replied. "What does it ask of you?"

Jonah sat with the question. He did not rush to answer.

Outside of work, Jonah noticed how his listening changed. He interrupted less. He offered fewer interpretations. He allowed conversations to end without closure.

Some people found this unsettling.

Others found it unexpectedly generous.

One evening, a former colleague called him, voice strained. "I don't know what to do," she said. "Everything feels wrong, and everyone wants me to choose anyway."

Jonah listened.

"I can't fix this," she said finally.

Jonah felt the familiar reflex rise—and settle.

"Then don't try to," he said gently. "Try staying honest instead."

There was a long pause on the other end of the line.

"Thank you," she said finally. "I needed someone not to rush me."

After the call ended, Jonah sat quietly, noticing how the same work continued to find him even without institutional permission. The difference now was that he no longer believed it had to be contained, measured, or sanctioned to matter.

He thought again of Claire.

Of how their time together had ended not with healing, but with recognition. Of how the system had withdrawn when the work stopped producing acceptable outcomes.

He understood now that care which refuses to fix exposes fault lines.

It reveals what institutions are willing to hold—and what they require individuals to carry alone.

One afternoon, Jonah returned to the old building to retrieve a box he had left behind. The hallway looked the same. The lights hummed softly. The conference room where he had met Claire stood empty, the door slightly ajar.

He paused there, memory pressing close.

He did not regret staying as long as he had.

He did not regret leaving when he could no longer stay without compromise.

What he regretted was how rarely the work had been named for what it was: not intervention, not treatment, not progress—but witness.

Jonah closed the door gently and carried the box to his car.

Driving away, he felt the weight of unresolved stories settle into him—not as burden, but as responsibility he could choose how to carry.

What couldn't be fixed had taught him something essential.

That care is not proven by improvement.

That faithfulness does not require resolution.

That staying, even temporarily, can matter deeply—especially when no one else will.

Jonah did not know where his path would lead next. He only knew that he would no longer confuse usefulness with truth, or urgency with love.

Some wounds, he had learned, do not heal.

They ask to be honored.

And some forms of care are defined not by what they accomplish, but by what they refuse to erase.

He started the engine and pulled into traffic, the road opening ahead of him without promise or plan.

It was enough—for now—that he knew how to remain present without fixing, and how to leave without pretending the work was done.

What couldn't be fixed had changed him.

And that change, he knew, would shape whatever care he offered next—quietly, imperfectly, and with eyes open to the cost.

Time passed in a way Jonah did not expect.

Without the familiar rhythm of case notes and follow-ups, days felt wider, less contained. He noticed how often he reached instinctively for his calendar, as if meaning might be scheduled. When it wasn't, he felt briefly unmoored.

This, too, was part of the injury.

He had spent years inside a system that equated care with momentum. Even now, free of its demands, he felt the pull of usefulness—an almost moral urgency to justify his time, to show that something was happening.

Nothing was.

And yet, something was settling.

Jonah began to recognize how deeply the expectation to fix had shaped him. He noticed it when friends spoke of difficulty and he felt the reflex to offer insight. He noticed it in himself when quiet moments stirred anxiety rather than rest.

He was learning, slowly, how to stay without producing.

One afternoon, he attended a small gathering of former colleagues. The conversation drifted, eventually, toward work. Names surfaced. Situations were referenced carefully, stripped of identifying detail but heavy with implication.

Someone mentioned Claire—not by name, but clearly.

"That situation was unfortunate," a colleague said. "I hope she found closure."

Jonah felt the familiar tightening.

He chose his words deliberately. "I don't think closure was the right question."

The group fell quiet.

"What do you mean?" someone asked.

Jonah hesitated. He knew this moment well—the invitation to translate, to explain in ways that would make discomfort manageable.

"I think what happened to her couldn't be resolved without denying what she knew to be true," he said. "And asking for closure would have required her to do that."

There was an uneasy pause.

"Well," someone said finally, "we all have to move on at some point."

Jonah nodded. "Yes," he said. "But moving on and moving past aren't the same thing."

No one responded.

The conversation shifted soon after. Jonah felt the familiar isolation rise—not sharp, but quietly clarifying. He understood now that this language would always sound excessive, inconvenient, unnecessary to those who had not lived inside the tension.

He did not resent them.

He simply knew where he stood.

That evening, Jonah went for a long walk as dusk settled in. He passed houses with lights glowing warmly behind drawn curtains. He wondered how many private reckonings were happening behind those doors, unseen and unnamed.

He thought about Claire again.

He had not heard from her in some time. He hoped that was a sign of steadiness rather than disappearance. He reminded himself that accompaniment was not ownership.

Still, he felt the ache of not knowing.

Weeks later, an envelope arrived in the mail. Jonah recognized Claire's handwriting immediately. His hands stilled as he opened it.

Inside was a short note.

I wanted you to know that I'm still carrying the truth of what happened—but I'm no longer carrying it alone. I've found a small circle of people who don't need me to explain it away. That has changed everything.

Jonah read the note twice, then once more.

He sat quietly for a long time afterward, the words settling into him like a benediction.

This, he realized, was repair—not resolution, not healing, but relocation. The weight had not disappeared. It had been shared.

That night, Jonah wrote for the first time in months. Not notes. Not reports. Just words.

Care does not always move pain forward, he wrote.

Sometimes it makes room for pain to stop moving at all.

The sentence surprised him.

He thought again of the system he had left—the way it required motion, decisions, outcomes. He saw now how deeply that requirement shaped what kinds of care were allowed.

Stillness had been suspect.

Witness had been tolerated only briefly.

In the weeks that followed, Jonah began to imagine a different way of working—one not defined by institutional permission, but by moral clarity. He did not yet know what form it would take. He did not rush to name it.

He was learning that not every future needed articulation.

One afternoon, he ran into his former supervisor at the grocery store. The conversation was polite, brief.

"I hear you're doing well," she said.

Jonah smiled. "I'm doing honestly," he replied.

She nodded, uncertain how to receive that.

As they parted, Jonah felt no resentment. Only distance.

He understood now that systems rarely mean harm. They simply organize care around what they can tolerate.

What they cannot tolerate, they outsource.

Jonah had been one of the places that outsourcing landed.

Now, without that role, he felt both lighter and more exposed. He carried fewer stories, but he carried them more consciously.

One evening, sitting alone at home, Jonah reflected on how his understanding of faithfulness had changed.

He no longer believed it was measured by effectiveness. Or endurance. Or outcomes.

Faithfulness, he was learning, had something to do with refusal—the refusal to translate suffering into something palatable, the refusal to offer hope that required distortion, the refusal to rush toward meaning when meaning had not yet earned trust.

He did not know whether this would make him employable in familiar ways.

He knew it made him honest.

As winter approached, Jonah began volunteering one afternoon a week at a local drop-in center. There were no case files, no reports. Just coffee, conversation, and long stretches of unremarkable time.

One day, a woman sat across from him and said, "Everyone keeps telling me to let it go."

Jonah looked at her gently. "What if you don't have to?"

She stared at him, startled.

They sat together in silence after that.

Jonah felt the familiar ache—and the familiar steadiness.

What couldn't be fixed continued to find him. Not as a burden, but as a calling he no longer needed permission to answer.

He had learned something essential.

That care is not defined by what it accomplishes.

That healing is not the only measure of love.

That staying, even briefly, can change the shape of suffering—without resolving it.

Jonah did not know how long this way of living would sustain him. He did not know what it would cost him over time.

What he knew was this:

He would no longer trade integrity for approval.

He would no longer confuse fixing with faithfulness.

He would no longer disappear into roles that required him to deny what he saw.

Some wounds would remain.

Some stories would not end cleanly.

And some forms of care would always look insufficient to those who needed closure more than truth.

Jonah accepted that now.

He stood by the window as snow began to fall, the world outside quiet and unresolved.

He felt no urge to make meaning of it.

He simply stayed.

And that, at last, felt like enough.

Jonah did not come to think of the story with Claire as unfinished.

That word implied something waiting to be completed, resolved, closed. Over time, he learned to think of it instead as uncontained—a truth that refused the shape of an ending and therefore continued to live.

That realization changed how he carried it.

Months had passed since her letter, and he had resisted the urge to check in again. Not out of indifference, but out of respect. Care, he was learning, did not always require continuation. Sometimes it required restraint—the willingness not to reinsert oneself to soothe one's own lingering concern.

Still, he thought of her often.

He thought of the conference room with its bland neutrality, of the coffee mug gone cold in her hands, of the way her voice steadied when she was finally told that fixability was not the measure of worth. Those memories did not ache the way they once had. They had settled into him as something quieter, more durable.

A kind of moral memory.

One afternoon, Jonah was invited to speak to a small group of graduate students preparing for ministry. The invitation surprised him; his name no longer circulated widely. Still, he accepted.

They gathered in a circle, notebooks open, eyes earnest. Someone asked a question Jonah recognized immediately.

"How do you know when you've done enough?" the student asked. "When care has actually helped?"

Jonah paused longer than usual.

"I don't think care proves itself the way we want it to," he said finally. "I think it proves us."

The students waited.

"When we rush toward outcomes," he continued, "we often end up serving our anxiety rather than the person in front of us. Sometimes care helps by making things better. Sometimes it helps by refusing to make them smaller."

A student frowned slightly. "But what if nothing changes?"

Jonah nodded. "Then the question becomes whether we're willing to stay honest anyway."

Afterward, a student approached him quietly. "No one's said that to us before," she said. "Usually we're taught to move people along."

Jonah smiled faintly. "You will be rewarded for that," he said. "Until you aren't."

Walking home that evening, Jonah felt the familiar weight settle again—not as burden, but as responsibility. He understood now that what he had learned with Claire was not situational knowledge. It was vocational truth.

Some forms of care would always place him at odds with systems that needed resolution more than witness.

He accepted that.

In the spring, Jonah ran into Claire by chance at a community event. They recognized each other instantly, a moment of stillness passing between them before either spoke.

She looked well. Not healed, not triumphant—simply grounded.

They exchanged a few words, nothing heavy. She mentioned a new rhythm of life, people who knew her story without demanding its conclusion. Jonah listened, grateful for the ordinariness of the exchange.

Before they parted, she said, "I don't think about what happened the same way anymore."

Jonah waited.

"It's still true," she continued. "But it doesn't define everything. Because no one's trying to fix it."

Jonah nodded. "I'm glad."

As she walked away, Jonah felt no urge to follow, no sense of unfinished business pulling at him. The care they had shared had reached its natural limit—not by resolution, but by sufficiency.

That felt right.

Later that year, Jonah declined a position that would have returned him to a familiar institutional role. The work was meaningful, the offer generous. But he recognized the conditions immediately—the subtle expectation that he would translate complexity into clarity, injury into narrative, patience into progress.

He declined without resentment.

Instead, he continued the quieter work that had found him—listening without agenda, staying present without promise, trusting that care did not need institutional endorsement to be real.

People still asked him what he did.

He learned to answer differently now.

"I stay with people," he said. "Sometimes that's all."

Some nodded, understanding more than they could articulate. Others smiled politely and changed the subject.

He no longer needed their approval.

One evening, Jonah sat again by the window as dusk settled in, watching the world grow indistinct at the edges. He thought about all the times he had believed faithfulness required him to produce something—to justify presence with outcome.

He no longer believed that.

Faithfulness, he understood now, was often defined by what one refused to do: refuse to rush, refuse to explain away, refuse to substitute movement for truth.

What couldn't be fixed had taught him that.

It had also taught him that some stories end not with healing, but with permission—the permission to stop striving for coherence, to live honestly inside what remains broken.

Jonah breathed deeply, feeling the quiet settle around him.

He knew there would be other stories like Claire's. Other moments when he would be asked, implicitly or explicitly, to make something whole that could not be made whole without violence to truth.

He knew the cost of resisting that pressure.

He also knew the cost of complying.

The weight he carried now was not lighter than before.

But it was chosen.

And that, he had learned, made all the difference.

Outside, night had fallen fully. Jonah turned off the light and let the darkness be what it was—unresolved, spacious, real.

What couldn't be fixed had not been erased.

It had been honored.

And that, finally, felt like care.

STORY 10

The Cost of Leaving Well

THE DECISION HAD ALREADY been made.

That was the strangest part.

David realized it one morning while standing at the kitchen sink, watching steam rise from his coffee. There was no drama in the moment, no sense of finality. Just a quiet recognition that the question he had been circling for months no longer felt open.

He was leaving.

Not in anger. Not in collapse. Not because he could no longer endure.

Because staying now required a story he could not tell truthfully.

That clarity did not bring relief. It brought weight.

David still showed up every day. He led meetings, returned emails, preached with care. From the outside, nothing had changed. Colleagues still spoke to him about next year, about long-term plans, about the work ahead.

He listened without correcting them.

He knew how much institutions relied on the illusion of continuity.

The hardest part was not deciding to leave. It was deciding how to leave without lying.

He had already heard the acceptable explanations. Burnout. A new call. Personal reasons. A season of discernment leading elsewhere. Each one offered a way out that preserved everyone's comfort—including his own.

Each one erased the truth.

The truth was not that he was tired, though he was.

Not that he had lost faith, though it had changed.

Not that he had been wronged in a way that could be summarized cleanly.

The truth was that he had been asked, repeatedly and quietly, to carry contradictions he could no longer hold without disappearing.

That truth did not fit on a farewell card.

One afternoon, David sat with his notebook open, drafting and deleting the same paragraph again and again. Every version softened something essential. Every honest sentence felt too sharp, too destabilizing.

He understood now why so many people left quietly.

Honesty had collateral damage.

Later that week, he met with a trusted colleague, someone who had been in the system longer than he had. They spoke easily at first, then carefully.

"I'm thinking of leaving," David said.

The colleague nodded, unsurprised. "I wondered when you would."

David waited.

"You've done good work," the colleague continued. "You should leave cleanly. Let it be about rest, or calling. Don't make it harder than it needs to be."

David felt the words settle heavily.

"Cleanly," he repeated.

"Yes," the colleague said gently. "For everyone's sake."

David nodded, understanding exactly what was being offered: protection, continuity, blessing without disruption.

And silence.

That night, he slept poorly. He dreamed of standing at a doorway, people behind him urging him to go, people ahead watching carefully to see how he would explain himself. When he opened his mouth, no sound came out.

He woke with his jaw clenched.

Over the following days, David noticed how often people reassured him without knowing it. "You've earned this." "You don't owe anyone explanations." "It's okay to take care of yourself."

All true. All incomplete.

What he owed himself was not rest.

It was coherence.

The exit interview loomed, an appointment framed as support. David knew how it would go. He would be asked what led him here. He would be encouraged to speak positively, to name gratitude, to bless the future.

He could do all of that.

The question was whether he would allow that to be the whole story.

When the day came, David sat across from two leaders he respected. The conversation began warmly. They thanked him for his service, praised his steadiness, acknowledged his contributions.

Then one of them asked, "Can you help us understand what led to this decision?"

The room felt very still.

David took a breath.

"I want to be careful," he said slowly. "Because I don't want to harm this place."

Both nodded.

"And I also don't want to leave behind a story that isn't true."

They waited.

"I didn't come to this because I was burned out," he continued. "Or because I stopped believing in the work. I came to it because over time, I found myself repeatedly choosing between honesty and harmony. And harmony kept winning."

The words hung in the air.

One leader shifted slightly. "That tension is part of leadership," she said carefully.

"Yes," David replied. "For a while."

Silence again.

"What I'm saying," he continued, his voice steady now, "is that staying began to require me to speak less truthfully than I could live with. Leaving is the only way I know to stop that from happening."

No one interrupted him.

When the meeting ended, they thanked him again. They did not argue. They did not affirm. They said they would process what he had shared.

Walking to his car afterward, David felt exposed and oddly calm. He knew the cost of what he had said. He also knew he could not take it back.

The announcement followed a week later. It was brief, gracious, careful. It named transition, gratitude, blessing.

It did not name truth.

David understood why.

On his last Sunday, he stood at the door greeting people as he always had. They hugged him, thanked him, wished him well. Many said, "You'll be missed."

A few asked, quietly, "Why now?"

David answered gently, without evasion.

"Because it was time," he said. "And because staying any longer would have asked too much of me."

Some nodded, understanding more than he had expected. Others smiled politely and moved on.

As the building emptied, David stood alone in the sanctuary. The light fell softly across the familiar space. He felt affection rise, and grief, and something steadier beneath them both.

Leaving well, he was learning, did not mean leaving clean.

It meant leaving without erasing yourself.

He turned off the lights and closed the door behind him.

The cost would come later—in misunderstandings, in cooled relationships, in stories told without him in the room.

He accepted that.

What he carried with him now was not certainty or relief.

It was alignment.

And that, he knew, was worth the price.

The days after the announcement were stranger than David expected.

Not harder—just oddly dissonant.

People treated him as if he were already gone and still fully present at the same time. Conversations softened around him. Decisions were deferred. Plans were discussed with an unspoken asterisk. He noticed how often sentences trailed off when he entered a room.

He had become temporary.

That status carried its own etiquette. People were kind, careful, almost reverent. Gratitude flowed freely. Conflict avoided him. No one wanted to burden someone who was "on their way out."

David understood the instinct.

He also felt its cost.

One afternoon, a colleague stopped by his office, leaning in the doorway with an expression that mixed warmth and caution.

"I just wanted to say," she began, "I really admire how you're handling this. Leaving with grace."

David smiled faintly. "Thank you."

She hesitated, then added, "It's such a gift to everyone when someone doesn't make their departure. . . complicated."

The word landed gently and sharply at the same time.

"Complicated," David repeated later, alone.

He wondered when truth had come to be understood as excess.

As his final weeks unfolded, David noticed how the institution began to metabolize his leaving. Responsibilities were reassigned. His name was removed from agendas. Future plans were revised as if he had always been provisional.

The system adapted quickly.

This, too, he understood.

What unsettled him was how easily his moral struggle disappeared in the process. The questions that had pressed him toward leaving—about honesty, complicity, and silence—found no place to land once he was framed as a transition rather than a witness.

He wondered whether that was inevitable.

At a farewell gathering, someone offered a toast. It was generous, affectionate, rehearsed. David listened as his work was summarized, his steadiness praised, his impact named in safe, celebratory language.

He felt gratitude.

He also felt the absence of something essential.

Afterward, a younger colleague approached him quietly.

"I hope this isn't inappropriate," she said, "but I wanted to thank you for what you said in that meeting."

David looked at her, surprised.

"The one where you talked about choosing between honesty and harmony," she continued. "I've been thinking about that a lot."

David nodded slowly. "I'm glad."

"I didn't know we were allowed to think about it that way," she said.

Allowed.

The word stayed with him.

In the final week, David cleared out his office slowly. Each book he placed in a box carried a memory. Each folder reminded him of decisions made carefully, compromises accepted gradually.

He paused over one file in particular—an old project that had stalled not because it lacked merit, but because it asked questions no one wanted to pursue. He realized, with a quiet ache, that his leaving was in some ways the continuation of that project.

Truth unfinished.

On his last day, David locked the office door and stood for a moment in the hallway. People passed by, offering hugs, last words, well-wishes.

Someone said, "You'll always be part of this place."

David smiled. He did not correct them.

Walking out to the parking lot, he felt the weight of finality settle more fully now. Not sadness exactly—something closer to gravity.

At home that evening, the house felt unfamiliar. He sat at the kitchen table, the same place where clarity had first arrived, and allowed himself to feel what he had held at bay for weeks.

Grief surfaced first.

Not just for what had been lost, but for what had never been possible. For the conversations that could not be had. For the truths that could not be spoken without cost.

He felt anger too—not hot, not explosive, but steady. Anger at how often integrity had been framed as inflexibility. At how silence had been rewarded as maturity.

He let the feelings come without translating them into lessons.

Over the next days, David noticed a subtle but persistent anxiety rise. Without the structure of the role, without the language that had once given his days shape, he felt exposed. He wondered who he was now, stripped of the story others told about him.

People asked what was next.

He answered honestly. "I don't know yet."

Some looked uncomfortable. Others relieved.

He realized how rarely that answer was permitted.

One evening, he ran into a former congregant at the grocery store. They greeted each other warmly, exchanged small talk. As they were about to part, she said, "I was sorry to hear you were leaving. You seemed . . . steady."

David considered the word, then nodded. "I was."

She hesitated. "Were you okay?"

The question caught him off guard.

"Yes," he said slowly. "And no."

She smiled sadly, as if she understood more than he expected. "I hope you're okay now."

"I'm becoming honest," David replied. "That feels like the right direction."

That night, he lay awake thinking about what it meant to leave well.

It was not, he realized, about minimizing disruption or preserving comfort. It was about refusing to trade coherence for approval.

Leaving well meant accepting misunderstanding.

It meant allowing others to simplify your story.

It meant resisting the temptation to justify yourself endlessly.

As weeks passed, David noticed something unexpected.

He felt more present.

Conversations no longer required calculation. Silence no longer felt strategic. He spoke when something mattered and let it go when it didn't.

The moral weight he had carried had not lifted.

But it had shifted.

It no longer pressed him inward, forcing contraction. It moved outward now, shaping how he listened, how he chose, how he named what he would and would not do.

One afternoon, David opened his notebook and wrote:

Leaving did not solve the injury.

It stopped requiring me to carry it quietly.

The sentence felt true.

He did not know what work awaited him. He did not know whether he would ever return to a similar role. He knew only that whatever came next would need to make room for the truths he could no longer abandon.

Leaving well, he was learning, was not a moment.

It was a practice.

One that would continue long after the door had closed, long after the blessing had been spoken, long after the system had moved on.

The cost was real.

But so was the freedom.

And for the first time in a long while, David trusted himself to bear what came next—without pretending it was lighter than it was.

David learned quickly that leaving did not end the work of interpretation.

It intensified it.

In the weeks after his departure, fragments of conversation reached him through indirect channels—comments relayed by friends, questions asked in his absence, small narratives forming to explain what had happened. None were hostile. Most were generous. All were incomplete.

He recognized the pattern with a familiar ache.

Institutions do not like ambiguity. When someone leaves without a clean reason, meaning rushes in to fill the gap.

David resisted the urge to correct the record. He knew how that game went. Clarification invited defense. Defense invited minimization. Minimization invited the quiet rewriting of what had been said.

He chose restraint.

Still, restraint had a cost.

One afternoon, a former colleague called him unexpectedly. The tone was friendly, careful.

"I hope this isn't awkward," the colleague began. "I just wanted to check in. There's been some confusion."

David listened.

"Some people are saying you left because you were unhappy," the colleague continued. "Others think you were frustrated with leadership. I've even heard burnout mentioned. I just wondered. . . is there anything you want me to clarify if your name comes up?"

David closed his eyes briefly.

He appreciated the care behind the question. He also felt the familiar pressure—to offer a version of the story that could circulate safely.

"I don't think clarification will help," he said gently. "What I shared was already as honest as it could be without becoming harmful."

There was a pause.

"So you're okay with people misunderstanding?" the colleague asked.

David considered the question carefully.

"I'm not okay with it," he said. "But I'm willing to tolerate it."

After the call ended, David sat quietly, feeling the weight of that choice settle into him. Misunderstanding was not a failure of communication. It was the price of refusing to simplify.

He wondered how often he had once encouraged others to accept that price without fully understanding what it cost.

Over time, David noticed his anger softening—not disappearing, but loosening its grip. What replaced it was something quieter and more complex: sadness for the limits of systems he still loved, and compassion for people who needed stories to be cleaner than reality allowed.

He did not excuse the harm.

He contextualized it.

One evening, David met a former congregant for coffee. The meeting was informal, unplanned. They spoke of ordinary things at first—work, family, the slow rhythms of life.

Eventually, the congregant leaned forward.

"I hope you don't mind me asking," she said, "but was leaving. . . necessary?"

David looked at her, surprised by the care in the question.

"Yes," he said simply.

She nodded, then hesitated. "I've been thinking about something you once said," she continued. "About truth not always being loud. I think I understand it better now."

David smiled faintly. "I'm glad."

"What do you do," she asked, "when telling the truth costs more than staying quiet?"

David took a moment.

"You decide what kind of cost you're willing to carry," he said. "And which one will cost you yourself."

The words surprised him with their clarity.

Walking home afterward, David realized that leaving had not resolved his moral questions. It had relocated them. Instead of being compressed inside institutional boundaries, they now unfolded across relationships, memories, and future choices.

That felt truer.

Months passed. David began tentative new work—nothing grand, nothing clearly defined. He taught a class. He offered consultation. He listened more than he spoke.

He noticed how often people arrived carrying similar stories: long seasons of adaptation, quiet self-censorship, the slow erosion of agency disguised as maturity.

He did not rush them toward leaving.

He did not romanticize staying.

He helped them name the cost honestly.

One evening, alone again at the kitchen table, David returned to the notebook that had accompanied him through the decision to leave. He reread earlier entries—uncertain, circling, heavy with restraint.

He added a new line.

Leaving well does not protect you from grief.

It protects you from disappearance.

The sentence felt earned.

David understood now that departure did not absolve him of responsibility. It sharpened it. He was accountable now not just for what he said, but for what he modeled—for whether his leaving became another story of quiet withdrawal or a living witness to moral seriousness.

He did not always succeed.

Some days, he wished he had left more cleanly, with fewer ripples, fewer questions trailing behind him. Other days, he was grateful for every unresolved edge.

The edges were where truth still breathed.

Late one night, David received a message from someone he barely knew—a brief note thanking him for naming something that had long gone unnamed. The message was simple, unadorned.

It mattered more than he expected.

He realized then that leaving well was not about controlling the narrative.

It was about relinquishing it.

Trusting that whatever truth needed to travel would do so without his supervision.

As the year turned, David felt something like steadiness settle into place. Not certainty. Not closure.

Alignment.

He had not found a new institution to belong to. He had not replaced the old one with something better.

He had, however, stopped asking himself to live inside a story that required his silence.

That, he knew now, was not a small thing.

Leaving well was not heroic.

It was costly, incomplete, and ongoing.

It required patience with misunderstanding, tolerance for loneliness, and a willingness to let faithfulness look inefficient.

David accepted that.

He did not know how his story would be told in the long run. He suspected it would be simplified, softened, perhaps forgotten.

What mattered was that he could live inside it without shrinking.

As he closed his notebook and turned off the light, David felt the familiar mixture of grief and gratitude settle once more.

The cost of leaving well was real.

So was the gift.

And for now, that was enough.

David had underestimated how much leaving would reorder his sense of time.

Inside the institution, time had been thick with expectation. Meetings followed meetings. Decisions created momentum. Even waiting had a shape to it—a discernment process, a season, a timeline that implied eventual clarity.

Outside it, time loosened.

Days were no longer justified by usefulness. Weeks passed without markers. David found himself measuring time not by outcomes but by attentiveness—how present he felt in conversation, how honestly he responded to questions, how often he noticed himself bracing for approval that no longer mattered.

The quiet was unsettling at first.

Then it became instructive.

One morning, David woke with the old instinct to check his email immediately, a reflex honed by years of responsiveness. He caught himself mid-reach and paused. The urge felt less like responsibility now and more like habit—an echo of a role he no longer occupied.

He let the phone remain where it was.

In the space that followed, a question surfaced unbidden: What am I allowed to want now?

It startled him how difficult it was to answer.

Wanting, he realized, had long been disciplined by institutional need. Desire had been filtered through feasibility, optics, and impact. Even prayer had learned to sound strategic.

Now, with no audience to reassure and no structure to appease, desire felt unformed—present but uncertain.

David sat with that uncertainty longer than he would have before.

He noticed how often people he met wanted reassurance from him. They asked how he was doing, but what they meant was whether leaving had been worth it. Whether alignment compensated for loss. Whether the cost had been justified.

He answered carefully.

"I'm not relieved," he would say. "But I'm not divided anymore."

Some nodded, satisfied. Others looked disappointed, as if hoping for a clearer moral equation.

David understood. The culture preferred tidy math: sacrifice in, freedom out. He was living something slower and more ambiguous.

One afternoon, he attended a service at a church he had no connection to. He slipped into a back pew, anonymous and unencumbered. The liturgy was familiar, the words worn smooth by repetition.

As the congregation confessed together, David felt something shift in his chest. The language of confession—what we have done and left undone—landed differently now. He realized how often he had spoken those words while privately calculating what could and could not be admitted in real life.

Now, there was no calculation.

He confessed quietly—not aloud, not dramatically—but with a clarity he had not known before. Not sins of intent, but sins of accommodation. Places where he had stayed silent longer than he should have. Moments where harmony had felt safer than truth.

He did not accuse himself.

He acknowledged himself.

After the service, David lingered outside, watching people greet one another warmly. No one knew who he was or what he carried. The anonymity felt oddly kind.

He thought about how often institutions required people to be legible in order to be trusted. Leaving had given him back the right to be partially unknown.

That felt like a gift.

Later that week, David met with a small group of peers—others who had left roles under similar conditions. The conversation moved carefully at first, circling shared experiences without pressing too hard.

Eventually, someone said what had been hovering.

"I keep wondering if I should have stayed longer," the person admitted. "Maybe if I'd tried harder, things could have changed."

David listened.

"I wonder that too sometimes," he said. "But I also know that staying wasn't neutral. It was shaping me."

The group fell quiet.

"Leaving didn't solve anything," another person added. "But it stopped something."

David nodded. "That's been true for me as well."

He realized then that leaving well was not about certainty. It was about refusal—the refusal to continue absorbing costs that could no longer be borne without distortion.

The cost did not vanish. It changed hands.

One evening, David found an old sermon manuscript tucked into a box he hadn't fully unpacked. He read it slowly, recognizing the careful phrasing, the deliberate omissions, the places where he had gestured toward truth without naming it.

He did not feel shame.

He felt tenderness for the person he had been—trying to be faithful inside constraints he did not yet know how to name.

He closed the manuscript and did not save it.

In the months that followed, David noticed a subtle shift in how he spoke. His words grew plainer. Less defensive. He stopped preemptively softening statements to avoid imagined pushback.

This did not make him more aggressive.

It made him clearer.

Some conversations ended sooner than they once would have. Others deepened unexpectedly. He learned to tolerate the discomfort of saying something true and letting the response be whatever it would be.

One night, he wrote again in his notebook:

Leaving well is not about having the last word.

It's about refusing to live inside a false one.

The sentence stayed with him.

David did not know what future institutional life, if any, awaited him. He did not romanticize independence or imagine himself immune to new forms of compromise.

He knew only that he would recognize the signs sooner now—the subtle invitations to silence, the praise that rewarded disappearance, the reassurance that everything difficult was simply part of the work.

He would listen differently.

Leaving had not made him purer.

It had made him more attentive.

As autumn approached, David felt the familiar rhythm of seasons settle in. Leaves changed. Light thinned. Life continued without asking whether his decision had been correct.

That felt right.

The cost of leaving well, he understood now, was not paid all at once. It was paid gradually—in moments of loneliness, in misrecognition, in the quiet work of rebuilding coherence without applause.

But the cost of staying had been cumulative too.

This cost, at least, was chosen.

David stood by the window one evening, watching dusk gather, and felt a quiet steadiness take hold. Not triumph. Not certainty.

Alignment.

He breathed deeply and let the day end without commentary.

Leaving well was still unfolding.

And for the first time, he trusted himself to stay with that unfolding—without rushing it toward resolution, without apologizing for its incompleteness.

That trust felt like the beginning of something durable.

Even if it never became easy.

What surprised David most was how often the leaving continued to ask something of him.

He had imagined departure as a kind of release—a boundary crossed, a door closed. Instead, he found that leaving initiated a new sequence of moral decisions, quieter but no less demanding. Without institutional cover, each choice now belonged entirely to him.

No committee to absorb responsibility.

No role to explain restraint.

No script to soften consequences.

The freedom was real.

So was the exposure.

David noticed this most clearly in conversation. When people learned where he had been and where he was now, they often leaned in, voices dropping instinctively.

"What really happened?" they would ask.

The question carried weight. It was not gossip-driven. It was hunger—for language, for validation, for permission to name experiences that had never been acknowledged aloud.

David felt the pull of that hunger.

He knew how much it mattered when someone finally told the truth.

He also knew how easily truth could become spectacle.

"I don't want to turn my leaving into a story that feeds someone else's discontent," he said once, gently but firmly. "That wouldn't be fair—to them or to the place I left."

The person nodded, disappointed but understanding.

David learned to speak carefully without becoming evasive. He named patterns rather than individuals. Pressures rather than betrayals. Costs rather than villains.

It was not neutrality.

It was discipline.

Still, there were moments when restraint felt like self-erasure in a different key. He wondered whether he was simply reproducing the same silence in new form—politeness masquerading as wisdom.

The line between integrity and accommodation was thinner than he liked.

One evening, David received an invitation to speak at a gathering focused on leadership resilience. The topic description included familiar language: sustainability, self-care, adaptive capacity.

He hesitated.

The invitation felt like recognition—and like temptation. He could accept and translate his experience into something palatable. He could speak of growth, lessons learned, the importance of boundaries.

All of that was true.

None of it named the injury.

David declined.

The decision cost him more than he expected. Not financially. Not professionally.

Relationally.

He realized how much belonging still flowed through shared language. By refusing to adopt the preferred frame, he made himself slightly unintelligible—less useful, less reassuring.

He wondered how many people learned to survive by becoming interpretable.

Over time, David's world grew smaller but denser. Fewer invitations. Deeper conversations. Less affirmation. More honesty.

He did not regret it.

But he did grieve the loss of ease.

One afternoon, David ran into a former leader he had worked closely with. They greeted each other warmly, spoke of neutral things. As they parted, the leader paused.

"I hope you know," he said carefully, "that I never thought you were wrong. I just didn't see a way forward."

David nodded. "I know."

The leader hesitated again. "Sometimes I wish you'd stayed."

David felt the old ache stir.

"Sometimes I wish that too," he said.

They stood for a moment longer, neither quite ready to leave. Then the leader added, almost to himself, "But I understand why you couldn't."

The words landed gently and heavily at once.

Walking away, David realized how rarely that kind of acknowledgment came. How much silence was sustained not by malice, but by fear—fear of what might unravel if one person's truth were fully received.

He felt compassion rise, tempered by resolve.

At home that evening, David returned to his notebook. He no longer wrote daily, but when he did, the words came with less effort.

Leaving well does not end the injury, he wrote.

It changes who is responsible for carrying it.

He paused, then added:

Sometimes that responsibility must be reclaimed.

In the months that followed, David noticed a subtle shift in how he imagined the future. He no longer thought in terms of roles or trajectories. He thought in terms of alignment and capacity.

What could he say yes to without contorting himself?

What costs was he willing to bear—and which ones were no longer his to absorb?

These questions did not yield clean answers.

But they yielded coherence.

One morning, David found himself teaching again—not in an official capacity, but informally, in a small setting with people eager to think deeply. The conversation moved slowly, thoughtfully. No one rushed toward application.

At one point, someone asked, "How do you know when leaving is faithful?"

David considered the question carefully.

"When staying requires you to deny what you know to be true," he said, "leaving may be the only way to stop the harm from continuing through you."

The room was quiet.

"And leaving well," he continued, "means refusing to turn that truth into a weapon—or to abandon it for comfort."

Afterward, several people lingered. One thanked him quietly. Another said nothing, but met his eyes with recognition.

David felt the familiar mixture of weight and steadiness return.

He understood now that leaving well was not a single ethical act, but an ongoing practice—one that required restraint, courage, and a tolerance for incompleteness.

There would be no moment when the cost was fully paid.

There would be no final vindication.

But there would be integrity.

And that, he had learned, was not a consolation prize.

It was the ground on which a different kind of faithfulness could stand.

As evening fell, David stepped outside and watched the light fade. The world did not ask him to explain himself. It did not require coherence.

It simply continued.

David breathed deeply and let himself stand inside that continuity—no longer trying to justify his place within it.

Leaving well had not made his life simpler.

It had made it truer.

And for now, that was enough to carry forward—quietly, imperfectly, and without apology.

David did not expect the leaving to become quieter.

He had imagined that distance would dull the edges, that time would blur what had been sharp. Instead, the clarity remained—not urgent, not raw, but steady. Like a scar that no longer ached but still shaped how the body moved.

He learned that clarity had its own discipline.

One afternoon, nearly a year after he had left, David was invited to attend a gathering connected to his former institution. The invitation was warm, informal, framed as reconnection rather than return.

He held it in his hands for a long time before responding.

Part of him wanted to go. Not out of nostalgia, but out of affection. These were people he had loved, places that had shaped him. Attending would signal that he bore no resentment, that bridges remained intact.

Another part of him recognized the quiet expectation embedded in the invitation: his presence would help confirm that everything had turned out fine. That whatever tension had existed belonged to the past, resolved by time and transition.

He declined.

Not abruptly. Not defensively.

Simply, honestly.

He wrote back thanking them for the invitation and explaining that attending would ask him to present a version of himself that no longer felt true.

The response was polite. Understanding. Brief.

David felt the familiar mixture of relief and loss settle in again.

Leaving well, he realized, often meant refusing reunion on false terms.

In the months that followed, David noticed how his internal life had changed. He no longer rehearsed conversations in advance, anticipating how much truth a room could tolerate. He no longer scanned for signs of disapproval before speaking.

This did not make him reckless.

It made him quieter in a different way—less defended, more deliberate.

When people asked about his past, he answered simply. He did not lead with explanation or apology. If they wanted more, he waited to see whether the question was rooted in care or curiosity.

He had learned the difference.

One evening, David sat with a small group discussing faith and vocation. The conversation turned, as it often did, to endurance—to how much one could absorb before something essential gave way.

Someone asked him, "How did you know it was time to leave?"

David paused.

"I didn't know all at once," he said. "I knew it because staying had begun to require a version of myself I couldn't live with. Leaving didn't solve that. It just stopped making me complicit in it."

The group fell quiet.

Afterward, a man lingered and said softly, "I think I'm getting close to that place."

David did not rush him toward a conclusion. He did not name leaving as the answer.

He said only, "Pay attention to what staying is asking of you."

As the seasons continued to turn, David felt a subtle gratitude grow—not for the injury itself, but for the seriousness it had forced upon him. He no longer believed that faithfulness was measured by longevity or by one's ability to endure quietly.

Faithfulness, he now understood, had something to do with refusing to normalize what deformed the soul.

That refusal did not require drama.

It required honesty.

One morning, David walked past the old building where he had once worked. He had not planned the route intentionally. The sight surprised him. He stopped for a moment, feeling memory rise without overwhelming him.

He did not feel bitterness.

He felt recognition.

This place had been real. His work there had mattered. And it had reached its limit.

Both could be true.

He did not go inside.

He continued walking.

That evening, David returned again to the notebook that had accompanied him through the leaving. He read the earliest entries—tentative, cautious, burdened by responsibility he could not yet name. He saw now how much he had been carrying before he ever acknowledged the cost.

He wrote one final entry.

Leaving well does not mean leaving without damage.

It means refusing to make damage disappear by denying it.

He closed the notebook and placed it on the shelf.

The story, he knew, would not resolve further. There would be no final chapter in which everyone understood, no moment when the cost was fully redeemed.

That was not a failure.

It was reality.

David had learned to live without requiring his choices to be validated by consensus. He had learned to tolerate the loneliness that sometimes accompanied integrity. He had learned that alignment was not comfort, but it was solid ground.

As night fell, he stood by the window once more, watching the lights come on across the neighborhood. Lives unfolding quietly, without explanation.

He felt no need to narrate his own.

The cost of leaving well remained real. It continued to shape his relationships, his work, his sense of belonging.

But it no longer felt like a wound he was obligated to heal.

It felt like a truth he had honored.

And that, finally, was enough.

David turned off the light and let the darkness settle—not as something to be resolved, but as something to be trusted.

The door had closed.

He had not disappeared.

And the life ahead of him, though uncertain, felt honest in a way it never had before.

Leaving well had not given him an ending.

It had given him a way to live.

CODA

What Remains Worth Bearing

THESE STORIES DO NOT ask to be solved.

They ask to be carried.

Across these lives, what repeats is not a single kind of harm or a shared set of circumstances, but a pattern of moral weight that accumulates when people are asked to remain faithful inside systems that cannot—or will not—tell the truth about their own limits. Some stay. Some speak. Some leave. None escape the cost.

If there is a temptation at the end of a book like this, it is to sort the stories into lessons. To decide which choices were right, which paths were wiser, which endings were more faithful. That temptation mirrors the very dynamics these stories resist: the urge to convert moral seriousness into clarity, ambiguity into instruction, witness into outcome.

That is not what these stories are for.

They are here to name what often remains unnamed. To make visible the injuries that occur not through cruelty, but through constraint. Not through malice, but through silence, process, loyalty, and the steady pressure to adapt.

They are here to remind us that moral injury does not always look like collapse. Often it looks like competence. Endurance. Respectability. Longevity.

And they are here to insist that faithfulness cannot be measured only by staying, or by leaving, or by fixing what cannot be fixed. Faithfulness is measured by whether a person is allowed to remain whole—able to speak truthfully, to act with integrity, to recognize cost without being asked to erase it.

Some of the people in these stories remained inside institutions that could not fully hold them. Others stepped away when staying required too much silence. None of these choices are offered as templates. All of them are offered as testimony.

What binds these stories together is not resolution, but courage: the courage to notice when harm has become normalized; the courage to name when care turns coercive; the courage to stop translating moral pain into something easier to bear for everyone else.

There is no promise here that truth will be rewarded. In many of these stories, it is not. Relationships cool. Narratives simplify. Institutions move on.

And yet.

Something endures.

What endures is the refusal to disappear quietly. The insistence that moral weight be acknowledged, even when it cannot be resolved. The choice to bear what is real rather than what is acceptable.

If you recognize yourself in these pages—whether as one who stayed, one who spoke, one who left, or one who learned how to witness without fixing—know this: the weight you carry is not evidence of failure. It is evidence of moral seriousness.

And moral seriousness matters.

It matters because communities that cannot bear truth will eventually ask individuals to carry it alone.

It matters because care that demands disappearance is not care.

It matters because faith that cannot tolerate honesty will eventually hollow itself out.

These stories do not tell you what to do.

They ask you to pay attention—to the costs you are absorbing, to the silences you are maintaining, to the ways your own integrity is being shaped, narrowed, or preserved.

They ask you to consider not just what you can endure, but what you should not have to.

In the end, what remains worth bearing is not the injury itself, but the truth it reveals: that faithfulness is not found in perfection or resolution, but in the quiet, costly commitment to remain honest—before God, before others, and before oneself.

That commitment does not always lead to belonging.

But it does lead to coherence.

And in a world—and a church—that often confuses silence with peace, coherence may be the most faithful gift we can offer.

This is not the end of the story.

It is simply where we stop pretending the weight is light.

Acknowledgments

THIS BOOK EXISTS BECAUSE of people who trusted me with what could not be fixed.

Some did so knowingly, others without realizing that what they were sharing would one day take narrative form. For that reason, I owe a debt I cannot fully repay—to those whose stories shaped these pages, and whose integrity required discretion. If you recognize yourself here, know that you have been honored, not exposed.

I am grateful to colleagues in ministry, judicatory life, counseling, and spiritual care who have stayed in difficult conversations long after clarity failed. Your willingness to resist easy explanations, to bear discomfort rather than erase it, and to name cost honestly made this work possible. You taught me that moral seriousness is not a deficit, but a form of faithfulness.

I owe particular thanks to those who read early drafts and offered careful, unsentimental feedback—especially when the temptation to resolve or instruct needed to be resisted. Your insistence that the stories remain truthful rather than tidy strengthened the book immeasurably.

To the pastors, elders, caregivers, and leaders who continue to labor within institutions they love, even when those institutions struggle to hold truth: your courage informed every page. This book is written with deep respect for the constraints you navigate and the costs you carry.

I am thankful as well for communities of faith that have shaped me—especially those that have taught me how to listen more carefully than I speak, and how to remain present without demanding answers. They have formed my understanding of care far more than success ever could.

Finally, I acknowledge those who taught me—sometimes painfully—that silence, endurance, and competence can conceal injury, and that naming what is real is not an act of disloyalty. It is an act of love.

Any failures of understanding or representation here are my own.

Acknowledgments

What truth this book carries belongs to those who bore the weight long before it was named.

About the Author

Rev. Gregory C. Smith, PhD is a retired Presbyterian pastor, clinical pastoral counselor, and writer whose work focuses on moral injury, faithfulness under constraint, and the hidden costs of institutional life. He holds a PhD in Clinical Pastoral Counseling and is a Licensed Clinical Pastoral Counselor and a Board Certified Grief and Trauma Therapist.

After decades of parish ministry and pastoral leadership, his work has increasingly centered on accompanying clergy and church leaders navigating moral injury, systemic strain, and vocational discernment. He brings together theological seriousness, clinical insight, and lived pastoral experience to name realities that are often misdiagnosed as burnout or personal failure.

Rev. Smith is the author of Bearing the Weight: Moral Injury, Public Witness, and Reformed Faithfulness and Beyond Burnout: A Clergy Care Handbook for Moral Injury and Faithful Discernment. His writing reflects a commitment to truthfulness over resolution and care that does not require disappearance.

He lives in Iowa and worships at Heartland Presbyterian Church in Clive.

www.ingramcontent.com/pod-product-compliance
Lightning Source LLC
LaVergne TN
LVHW050635100826
845148LV00011B/1877

* 9 7 9 8 3 8 5 2 7 7 8 4 1 *